Laurel dreamed of the day she met Jackson.

The summer afternoon party wasn't a typical event for either of them and later Laurel would think of what a cliché their meeting had been. Eyes meeting across a crowded room. Everyone else fading into a misty background. Her toes curling when he smiled. Sparks of sexual awareness coursing through them when their hands touched.

They had left the party together a short while later and went for a barefoot walk on the beach at sunset. The salty breeze tossed their hair and tugged at their clothes—clothes they had abandoned in a hidden nook. They had been daring and reckless and impetuous that night. By dawn the next morning, they knew they were in love.

She dreamed of that beach, of conversation and laughter, of passionate whispers and hoarse cries.

Of two young people so desperately in love that they had let their emotions sweep them into a life neither of them had been prepared for.

GINA WILKINS

is a bestselling and award-winning author who has written more than sixty-five books for Harlequin and Silhouette. She credits her successful career in romance to her long, happy marriage and her three "extraordinary" children.

Gina knows all too well the experience of sitting in an ICU with one of her children, and she drew heavily on those memories while writing this book, finding it a therapeutic exercise in many ways. Thankfully, her daughter has fully recovered, but Gina's sympathies will always go out to those parents who are struggling daily with that situation.

A lifelong resident of central Arkansas, Gina sold her first book to Harlequin in 1987 and has been writing full-time since. She has appeared on the Waldenbooks, B. Dalton and *USA TODAY* bestseller lists. She is a four-time recipient of the Maggie Award for Excellence, sponsored by Georgia Romance Writers, and has won several awards from the reviewers of *Romantic Times*.

LOGAN'S LEGACY

THE SECRET HEIR
GINA WILKINS

Published by Silhouette Books
America's Publisher of Contemporary Romance

Special thanks and acknowledgment are given
to Gina Wilkins for her contribution
to the LOGAN'S LEGACY series.

 SILHOUETTE BOOKS

ISBN 0-373-61392-X

THE SECRET HEIR

Be a part of

$\mathscr{L}$OGAN'S $\mathscr{L}$EGACY

*Because birthright has its privileges
and family ties run deep.*

Once crazy for each other, a husband and
wife lose their way. As an adorable little
boy reunites them, this couple learns that
sometimes love is meant to last a lifetime....

Jackson Reiss: Once he discovered his true
heritage, Jackson had a chip on his shoulder and
was blinded by resentment. But when his son
Tyler became ill, Jackson realized some things
took precedence—his child's health...and his wife
by his side.

Laurel Reiss: After a stormy upbringing, Laurel
gave everything to Jackson until circumstances
swept them into different orbits. With little Tyler in
trouble, Laurel devoted herself to his care...and felt
that strong passion toward Jackson re-emerge.

Jack Crosby: This mischievous patriarch had held
himself at a distance from his biological son. But as
a dire situation hit the Reiss household, would Jack
give his son the support he needed?

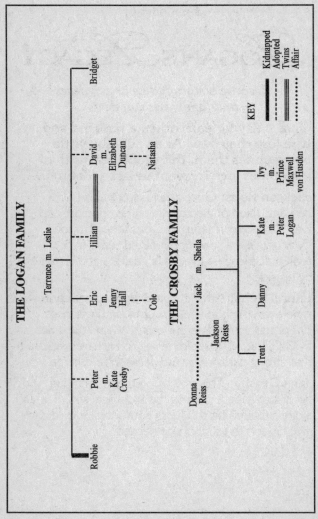

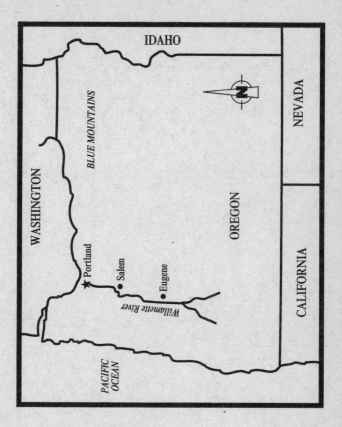

For my family—immediate and extended—
who have to live daily with the mood swings,
panic attacks, distraction and paranoia of the average
writer. Thank you for your love and your patience.

One

Laurel Phillips Reiss was a strong, competent, self-sufficient woman. Everyone who knew her said so. She could handle anything.

Anything except this.

Twisting a shredded tissue between her hands, she looked through her lashes at the man sitting in a nearby chair in the hospital waiting room. His sun-streaked blond hair was tousled from running his hands through it. Strong emotions darkened his blue eyes to navy and hardened his chiseled features to resemble granite. Years of manual labor had toned his broad-shouldered body. Jackson Reiss looked fit, tough and strong enough to overcome any adversity.

Except this one.

His eyes met hers. "Are you okay?"

She nodded, but even that silent response was a lie. She wasn't at all okay.

Other people sat in the waiting room, clustered in tight units as they waited for news of loved ones. Conversations swirled around them, the volume fluctuating from muted to rather loud. Occasional bursts of self-conscious, too-cheery laughter were followed by nervous silences. On the far side of the waiting room, a young woman cried softly. Laurel watched as a man gathered her into his arms to comfort her.

The green upholstered chairs in which Laurel and Jackson sat were crowded together so that their knees almost touched, but they made no effort to close even that small distance. Laurel's hands were in her lap, and Jackson's were fisted on his knees. A plain gold band gleamed on the ring finger of her left hand. His hands were bare, since jewelry could be dangerous on the construction sites where he spent most of his time.

There might as well have been a wall between them.

A dark-haired man who looked maybe ten years older than Laurel's twenty-six approached them with a respectful, slightly weary expression. He wore a white coat over a blue shirt and khakis. His tie was a riot of color. A nametag identified him as Michael Rutledge, M.D. "Mr. and Mrs. Reiss?"

Laurel surged to her feet as Jackson did the same. "How is Tyler?" she asked urgently. "What's wrong with him?"

"If you'll both follow me." He motioned toward a row of doors at one end of the waiting room. "We can talk privately in a conference room."

Laurel felt a band tighten around her heart. If he

wanted to talk to them in private, then something must really be wrong, she thought in despair. Wouldn't he have already reassured them if everything was fine?

Her body felt stiff and unresponsive when she tried to move. She stumbled a little, and Jackson reached out immediately to steady her. For only a moment, she allowed herself to sag against him, drawing on his strength. But then she squared her shoulders and stepped away from him. "I'm all right," she murmured.

Her husband nodded and shoved his hands in the pockets of the faded jeans he wore with battered work boots and a denim shirt. Dressed more colorfully in a red jacket and black slacks, Laurel moved a couple of steps ahead of Jackson as she followed the doctor into a small room with four straight-back chairs arranged around a round table.

A box of tissues sat on the table. A smudged white board hung on one wall, and a peaceful painting of mountains and clouds hung on another. A tall green plant stood in one corner; it needed water, Laurel noted automatically, focusing on inconsequential matters until she was certain she had her emotions under tight control.

"Please, Mrs. Reiss." Dr. Rutledge held a chair for her. "Sit down."

She would rather have stood, but she sank to the edge of the chair. Jackson took the seat beside her—close, but again without touching her. Both Laurel and Jackson kept their eyes on the doctor as he took a chair across from them. Laurel started to speak, but discovered that her throat was too tight. Hearing Jackson draw a deep breath, she let him ask the question that was paramount to both of them.

"What's wrong with our son?"

Before the doctor could reply, a forty-something woman with fiery red hair, a round, freckled face, and a plumply maternal figure knocked once and entered the room, carrying a thick file. "Sorry," she murmured to the doctor. "I got delayed."

"No problem." Dr. Rutledge stood upon the nurse's entrance. "Mr. and Mrs. Reiss, this is Kathleen O'Hara, the nurse practitioner who has been assigned to Tyler. She'll be your contact person who can answer all your questions during Tyler's treatment."

Nodding perfunctorily to the nurse, Jackson waited only until they were seated before saying again, "What's wrong with our son?"

Laurel tried to concentrate on the rather technical information the doctor gave them for the next ten minutes or so, but the words seemed to fly past her in a haze. She absorbed just enough to understand that her precious three-year-old son was suffering from a potentially fatal heart-valve defect.

"The good news is that we've caught the condition early," Dr. Rutledge assured them, leaning slightly toward Laurel as he spoke. "All too often the first sign of trouble is when a young person with this defect—usually a male in his late teens or early twenties—drops dead after participating in a rigorous sport. That's not going to happen with Tyler because we know what we're dealing with."

"You said he'll need a couple of operations. One now and one more as he grows." Jackson's voice was rather hoarse. Glancing his way, Laurel saw that the sun lines around his eyes and mouth had deepened, and that much of the color had drained from his tanned face. "How dangerous are those operations?"

"I won't lie to you. There's always a risk during surgery." The surgeon spent another few minutes outlining the possible complications, what Laurel had always thought of as the medical "C.Y.A." spiel. He spoke with practiced compassion, a speech he had obviously made many times before.

Laurel had to make an effort to sit still and listen quietly when every maternal cell within her was urging her to run screaming to Tyler's side, where she could gather him into her arms and protect him from harm. This wasn't just any sick child Michael Rutledge was discussing in such bewilderingly complex terms. This was Laurel's baby. The one perfect part of her life.

Jackson was the one who sprang to his feet, beginning to pace the small room with the barely restrained ferocity of a caged tiger. "How did this happen?" he demanded. "Was Tyler born with this condition or has something gone wrong since?"

"This is a congenital defect. He was born with it."

Was it *her* fault? Laurel had tried to take very good care of herself during her pregnancy, staying away from caffeine, alcohol and cigarette smoke, eating plenty of fruits and vegetables, taking her vitamins—everything she had been advised to do. Had she done something wrong, after all?

"The condition is almost always inherited," the doctor explained further. "The condition occurs most frequently in males. Perhaps one of you can remember uncles or cousins, even siblings who died of heart failure in childhood or early adulthood."

Laurel looked at Jackson, who was looking back at her in question. She shook her head. Her father had taken off when she was young, but she remembered him as a sports enthusiast who bragged about how healthy his family had always been.

Her mother's family was known for long life spans. Both of Laurel's maternal grandparents were still living back in Michigan, as far as she knew, though her extended family had been estranged since her mother had moved here to Portland, Oregon when Laurel was just a baby. Laurel's mother, Janice, had said often that she expected to live to a ripe old age, since everyone in her family did—even the ones who smoked and drank and ate anything they wanted, she had boasted.

Janice had died young, but that had been due to stupidity rather than heredity. Janice had been driving drunk after a party.

"I can't remember hearing anything like that about my mother's family or my dad's, but I'll ask them," Jackson said, pushing a hand through his hair again.

Laurel's hands clenched suddenly in her lap. "Does this mean that my husband could have the same defect? Is he also at risk?"

"I'm 31," Jackson reminded her. "I played football in high school and I've been doing construction work for years without a problem."

"Which is a good indicator, but a thorough physical examination certainly wouldn't hurt," the doctor advised.

Laurel and Jackson had grown apart during the past three years, but she didn't want to think about him being in danger. She was actually rather surprised by how strongly she had reacted when the possibility had entered her mind.

Now she concentrated fully again on her son. "When can I see Tyler?"

Dr. Rutledge pushed his chair away from the table and stood. "We're running a couple more tests, but he should be back in his room in a half hour or so. I'll send someone to the waiting room for you as soon as he's ready. In the meantime, Kathleen has several permission and release forms to discuss with you. She'll tell you more about what to expect during the next few weeks and answer any further questions for you. I'll be seeing you both again soon."

"Thank you," Jackson said.

Laurel could only nod. She found herself unable to thank the surgeon for giving her news that had shaken the very foundation of her life. If something went wrong…if she lost Tyler…

She couldn't even bear to think of that now.

"Dr. Rutledge has scheduled Tyler's surgery for seven-thirty Friday morning, the day after tomorrow," Kathleen began, opening the thick file to the first form. "Normally it would take a bit longer to arrange, but he had an unexpected opening and thought you might prefer to get this behind you."

Jackson nodded. "He was right."

"Good. Then we'll start preoperative evaluation this afternoon—chest X-rays, electrocardiogram, echocardiogram, oxygen saturation. Tomorrow you should be able to meet with the other members of Tyler's cardiology team—the anesthesiologist and the intensive-care staff who will take care of him after surgery. He'll be on a ventilator for several hours afterward, maybe overnight, until he's awake enough and his heart appears strong enough to discontinue the breathing assistance. We'll keep him here for seven to fourteen days, depending on how quickly he rebounds. You'll be fully briefed on recovery care before he leaves us."

Ventilator. Laurel gulped, barely hearing anything else the briskly professional woman said. The nightmare just kept getting more horrifying.

Jackson had several more questions for Kathleen, and Laurel tried to pay attention, but she had nothing to ask. She couldn't think clearly enough to form a coherent question.

After Jackson had signed all the forms—Laurel's hands were shaking too hard to hold a pen—the nurse closed her file. "I'll go check on Tyler. The two of you are welcome to use this room for a few more minutes if you need some private time. Someone will let you know if the conference room is needed."

Laurel could only nod again, clenching her jaw to hold back the tortured cry that seemed to be lodged in her throat.

Jackson watched the nurse let herself out of the conference room. The room was entirely too small. There seemed to be barely enough oxygen for two people. Tugging at the open collar of his denim shirt as though it were choking him, he turned to pace again, crossing the entire floor in four long strides.

His entire body practically vibrated with the need for action, the urge to do something to solve this crisis. That was his responsibility, wasn't it? To keep his family safe and happy. He hadn't been doing so well in the latter area lately, especially with his wife, but he had done his best to keep them safe. And now even that had slipped beyond his control.

What good was a father who couldn't protect his child?

Swallowing a sound that could have become a string of curses or a howl of anguish, he pushed his hands more deeply into his pockets and turned to look at Laurel. She sat on the edge of her chair, her back very straight, both hands in her lap, both feet on the floor. Her shoulder-length, dark-blond hair fell in neatly arranged layers, and her red jacket fit her slender frame perfectly. In contrast to that cheery tone, her lovely face was drained of color, so pale she could have been carved of ivory.

When he had met her almost four years ago, Laurel had been a laughing, ebullient, self-admitted party girl. Drawn to her spirit and her laughter, Jackson had swept her into a whirlwind courtship and a hasty marriage. Barely ten months later, their son was born.

Sometime during the course of their marriage, Jackson had realized that Laurel's laughter and chatter were as effective as any mask at hiding her true thoughts and feelings. As the months of their marriage passed, she had become quieter and more withdrawn from him. He could honestly say that she was even more of a stranger to him now than on the day they had met.

The one thing he knew without hesitation was that she adored their son. She had to be in agony now, just as he was.

He wished she would turn to him for comfort. That

was something useful he could do, at least, perhaps finding some reassurance for himself in the process. But in all the time he had known her, he had never heard Laurel ask for anything. Her rather fierce self-sufficiency had drawn him to her at the beginning, but for the past three years it had been slowly driving them apart.

He felt compelled to make the effort anyway. Moving to stand behind her chair, he rested a hand on her shoulder, feeling the tension vibrating in her muscles. "Laurel?"

She looked up at him. "Dr. Rutledge said Tyler should be fine after surgery."

Jackson suspected she was repeating the doctor's words as much to reassure herself as him. "Tyler will be fine, Laurel. Nothing's going to go wrong."

She swallowed visibly and nodded. Her fingers clenched so tightly in her lap that he heard a knuckle pop. "He's so little," she whispered, her sapphire-blue eyes filling with tears. "And they're going to cut him open…"

Acting on instinct, Jackson drew her somewhat roughly to her feet and into his arms. She stood stiffly there for a moment, and he began to wonder if she would push him away. But then she collapsed against him, her body wracked with shudders as she clung to the front of his shirt. She wasn't crying, exactly, he noted as he gathered her closer and rested his cheek against her soft hair, but her breath caught in ragged gasps that told him she was holding back sobs with an effort.

His protective-male instincts kicked into full force again. He wanted to promise her anything, do whatever it took to make their son well and ease Laurel's pain. If he could trade places with Tyler, he would do so in a heartbeat. If money would solve the problem, he would get it somehow, even if it meant working longer than the twelve- to sixteen-hour days he already put in.

It tormented him that there was absolutely nothing he could do. His child's well-being was in other people's hands now. He hated that.

The conference-room door opened and an attractive woman in her early fifties rushed in, followed closely by a stocky, worried-looking older man.

"Jackson!" Donna Reiss clutched his arm as Laurel moved abruptly away. "The receptionist told us you were in here. What's wrong with Tyler?"

Glancing quickly at Laurel, who had composed her face again into an inscrutable mask, Jackson knew their momentary bonding was over. Her thoughts were hidden from him now, as they so often were. Laurel didn't seem to need him just then, so he turned, instead, to the person who did.

Taking his mother's trembling hands, he squeezed comfortingly. "I'll try to explain what the doctor told us."

She clung to him, gazing up at him with both love and fear in her eyes. In contrast to Laurel, Donna always wore her emotions where everyone could see them. "Is he going to be okay?"

"He's going to need open-heart surgery, but the doctor seemed confident the condition is correctable."

"Open-heart surgery?" Donna repeated weakly. "Oh, no."

Feeling her sway a bit, Jackson helped her into a chair. "Dad, do you want to sit down?"

Carl Reiss shook his gray head and moved to stand behind his wife. Like Jackson, Carl preferred to be on his feet, ready to do whatever he was called upon to do.

"Tell us what's going on, Jay," he said simply, using the nickname he always called his son. And then he glanced at Laurel. "Maybe you should sit, Laurel. You look awfully pale."

"I'm fine, thank you." She crossed her arms more tightly over her chest and stood against one wall, as far away physically from the others as possible. And even farther away emotionally, Jackson thought.

Looking stricken anew, Donna turned in her chair to face her daughter-in-law. "Laurel, I'm sorry. I didn't mean to ignore you. It's just that I was so worried. But *you* must be frantic. Are you all right?"

"I'm fine, thank you." The words were exactly the same she had used to answer Carl, but, as always, her tone was just a shade cooler when she spoke to her mother-in-law.

Donna directed her attention back to Jackson. "Tell me everything."

He told her as much as he could remember, from the frantic call he had received from Laurel that morning through the talk with Dr. Rutledge. "They're running a few more tests now," he concluded. "We'll be notified as soon as we can see him."

One hand at her throat, Donna shook her head in disbelief. "Thank goodness Beverly is a former nurse's aide who recognized the signs that something was wrong! If it hadn't been for her, we might not have had any warning until it was too late."

Laurel moved abruptly toward the door. "Excuse me.

I need to…freshen up. Find me if they come for us," she added to Jackson on her way out.

Knowing she wouldn't want him to, he didn't try to follow her.

Closed into the dubious privacy of a ladies' room stall, Laurel finally let herself cry. She couldn't handle this, she thought. Anything else but this.

Maybe if she had been a better mother. More attentive. A perfect stay-at-home mom, like Donna Reiss had been. Then Laurel, rather than Tyler's nanny, would have been the one who had made note of the light-blue tinge around the boy's lips after he'd been running, or the slightly ragged edge to his breathing at times.

Despite all the times she had played with him, tickled him, run with him, Laurel had never seen the warning signs. It had taken a nurse's-aide-turned-nanny to realize that something was very wrong.

Laurel felt like such a failure as a mother—something she had feared since the day she had been told, to her shock, that she was pregnant. Still barely used to the idea of being a wife, she had almost panicked at the prospect of parenthood. What did she know about being a mother when she had never really had one herself?

For three years she had done the best she could at motherhood. She had read all the books, devoted herself to the role with an intensity that had overshadowed almost everything else in her life. Two years ago, after coming to the conclusion that she was hovering on the edge of clinical depression and would be a better mother if she felt a bit more personally fulfilled, she had returned to her job as a social worker. But even then she had tried to keep her hours reasonable, she reminded herself defensively. Certainly more reasonable than Jackson, who was rarely home.

Laurel had interviewed dozens of potential nannies, selecting the woman she had considered the best, even though Jackson had grumbled about the cost. It had taken the lion's share of Laurel's salary just to pay for child care, but despite Jackson's suspicions, she didn't really work for the money. She just needed to feel as if she was doing something worthwhile. Something that made her feel valuable and competent.

She should have been content with being a full-time wife and mother, she thought now. But, unlike her job, which inspired confidence in her abilities, those other roles left her feeling clueless. As Jackson's oh-so-perfect mother had just pointed out, it had taken a nanny even to realize that Tyler was seriously ill.

Was everyone judging her for not being the one to notice? Or was she the only one who found that so hard to forgive?

Knowing she had to emerge from the restroom eventually, she splashed cold water on her face, composing her expression as much as possible. The door opened before she touched the handle, and two older women walked in, both nodding greetings to Laurel as they passed.

She found her husband and his parents in the waiting room. Donna and Jackson sat on a vinyl-covered bench, Donna's head resting on her son's shoulder. Carl roamed restlessly from a stand of magazines to a saltwater aquarium, which held his attention for only a short while.

Laurel had never gotten to know her father-in-law very well. Almost ten years older than his wife, sixty-one-year-old Carl Reiss was a good-natured but quiet mechanic. His skin was weathered, his sandy-turned-gray hair thinning, and his brown eyes had a perpetual squint, as though from hours of peering into the sun.

Though very much like his father in mannerisms, Jackson was physically more like his mother. Both Jackson and Donna were blond—though Donna's color was artificially maintained now—and they had the same dark-blue eyes. Laurel had been told that Donna had once been drop-dead gorgeous, and even at fifty-two, she was still slim and striking. Jackson had definitely inherited his good looks from his mother.

Tyler was a blond, blue-eyed, miniature replica of his own father. But from whom had he received his tiny defective heart? Laurel couldn't help wondering with a catch in her throat.

Jackson stood when he saw Laurel approach. "You okay?"

She didn't bother lying to him again. "No word yet about when we can go to Tyler?"

"No. Not yet."

She turned toward the desk. "This is ridiculous. I want to see my baby."

Jackson moved after her, and for a moment she thought he was going to try to stop her. Instead, he took her arm and walked with her to the reception desk. "We'd like to see our son," he said to the efficient-looking woman sitting there.

"I'm sure you'll be called as soon as they're ready for you, Mr. Reiss."

"We're going in now," he said, moving toward the doors. "You can either call an escort, or we'll go find Tyler ourselves."

"Um, just a moment." The woman hastily picked up the receiver of the telephone on her desk. Moments later a stern-faced nurse appeared to escort them back.

Jackson Reiss had always had a way of getting what he wanted, Laurel thought with a touch of wistfulness.

Unfortunately, this seemed like the first time in almost four years that she and he had wanted the same thing.

Two

Tyler burst into tears the moment he saw his parents, and held out his little arms to Laurel. She scooped him up, snuggling her face into his neck. "See?" she said, her voice bright and bracing. "I told you Mommy and Daddy would be close by."

"Wanna go home."

"I know, baby." She shifted him more snugly onto her hip. His legs, bare beneath the thin, child-sized hospital gown, wrapped around her with a grip that let her know he wouldn't release her again without a struggle. "We have to stay here now, but Mommy's going to be right here with you, okay?"

"Wanna go home," Tyler repeated, his lip quivering as he looked to his father for reinforcement.

Jackson reached out to ruffle Tyler's fine, white-blond hair. "We'll take you home as soon as the doctor says it's okay, buddy."

A chocolate-skinned nurse with a riot of black curls around her appealing face hovered nearby. She nodded toward a deeply cushioned chair on one side of the private hospital room. "That chair converts into a single bed. One of you is welcome to spend the night here with Tyler."

A wooden rocker sat on the other side of the standard hospital bed on which Tyler had been sitting when Laurel and Jackson entered. Picking up the stuffed penguin Tyler had dropped on the bed, Laurel sat in the rocker with Tyler nestled in her lap. Leaving Jackson to talk with the nurse, she concentrated on cheering up her son.

"You and I are going to spend the night here, Tyler. Mommy will sleep right here beside your bed."

Tyler sniffed. "Angus, too?"

"Of course Angus, too." She patted the stuffed penguin's somewhat grubby head. "And look, we have a TV and a stack of cartoon movies. There are some of your favorites here. We'll watch one together, okay?"

Tyler nodded tentatively. Her promise that she would stay with him had reassured him somewhat, even if he was still clearly bewildered by what was going on.

Barely three, he was still too young to understand that even though he felt fine, there was something wrong with him that required medical intervention. To him, it must seem that one moment he had been playing with his toys and the next he'd been in the hospital being poked and prodded by strangers.

That was pretty much the way it felt to Laurel, too.

On the suggestion of Beverly Schrader, their nanny, Laurel had taken the morning off on this nice Thursday in early April to take Tyler for a medical checkup. Though she had tried to convince herself that Beverly was overreacting, she had mentioned to the pediatrician the symptoms Beverly had noted. The pediatrician had taken Beverly's observations seriously enough to run a few tests—and the next thing she'd known, Laurel had been sitting in the Portland General Hospital waiting room while Tyler was rushed to specialists.

She had tracked Jackson down on a construction job he was supervising. He had dropped everything and hurried to join her. And suddenly they were facing open-heart surgery.

It had all happened so fast that Laurel's head seemed to be spinning. No wonder little Tyler was confused.

She heard Jackson asking a string of questions of the patiently helpful nurse, but she didn't try to monitor that conversation. She figured Jackson would tell her later what she needed to know. For now she focused on her child.

"I'll be back at five with your dinner, Tyler," said the nurse, whose nametag identified her as Ramona. "Do you like spaghetti and applesauce?"

Tyler nodded, then added, "Like ice cream, too."

Ramona flashed a smile. "I'll see what I can do about that."

Left alone, Laurel and Jackson studied each other over Tyler's head. More at home in the chaos of a construction site, Jackson looked restless and uncomfortable in the sterile and studiously cheery setting of a hospital pediatric room.

"I should probably go get my parents," he said, glancing toward the door.

Laurel's arms tightened spasmodically around her son and words of protest rose instinctively in her throat, but she swallowed them and nodded. Jackson had every right to want his parents with him, just as they had a right to be close to their grandchild. She was being selfish to want to keep Tyler all to herself until this whole ordeal was over.

It was just that once the close-knit Reiss family was together, Laurel always felt like the outsider. Changing her surname to theirs hadn't made her one of them.

It wasn't that they had ever treated her badly. They had been nothing but politely gracious to her, just as they were to everyone outside the family. She knew much of the problem was hers. Since she hadn't been raised in a family like this, she had never quite known how to behave with them, resulting in her being a bit guarded around them.

Though adept at making small talk and swapping repartee with others, she'd turned stilted in the presence of Jackson's parents. Jackson, for one, had certainly noticed. He had accused her almost from the beginning of not liking his parents, and the more he had pushed her, the more defensive she had become. Especially when it came to his paragon of a mother.

Laurel had fifteen minutes alone with her son, and she savored every one of them. Though his vocabulary was limited, he managed to tell her about the people who had looked at him and done so many things to him. Laurel and Tyler had actually been separated for just over an hour, but it had seemed much longer to both of them. Tyler admitted he had rather liked nurse Ramona, but he was glad to be with his mommy again.

Snuggled into her arms, he stuck his left thumb into his mouth and allowed himself to relax, his eyelids getting heavy. Laurel rested her cheek on his silky blond hair and closed her own eyes, desperately wishing—

"There's my sweet baby." Donna Reiss rushed into the room on a wave of floral perfume and grandmotherly concern. She knelt beside the rocking chair and rested a trembling hand on Tyler's arm. "Gammy's here, darling, and so is Gampy. We're all going to take very good care of you."

"Gammy," Tyler murmured with a sleepy smile. But it was Laurel's heart he nestled closer to as he drifted into a restless nap.

It was almost eight o'clock that evening when Jackson convinced Laurel to leave the hospital room for a short break. Reminding her that she had missed lunch, he persuaded her to join him in the hospital cafeteria for a quick dinner. Tyler was sleeping, and Donna and Carl said they would stay with him until Laurel returned. They had already eaten, Carl having almost dragged Donna out of Tyler's room for forty-five minutes earlier.

Laurel had tried to talk Jackson into joining his parents then, but he had refused to eat until she did. Though she wasn't hungry, and she hated to leave her son even for that brief time, Laurel finally conceded because she knew Jackson needed the break.

The serving line closed at eight, so there weren't many diners left, and not much food, either. Laurel ordered a bowl of soup, Jackson a sandwich.

They carried their trays to a small table next to a glass wall that looked out over a beautifully landscaped courtyard bathed in soft lighting. Because she knew he would insist, Laurel forced herself to take a few bites of the soup.

"How is it?" he asked, looking up from his food.

"Rather cold," she replied with a shrug. "But it tastes fine." At least, she assumed it did. For all the attention she had paid to the soup, it could have tasted like wet sawdust.

Jackson finished his sandwich while she made a pretense of eating, both of them lost in their own thoughts. And then he pushed his plate aside, leaving the chips and pickle untouched. "I guess I wasn't as hungry as I thought."

Laurel set down her spoon. "Neither am I."

"You barely touched your soup. You'll need to eat to keep your strength up. We've got a tough time ahead."

"I'll eat. I'm just not hungry now."

He nodded and looked down at his hands, which were gripped together on the table in front of him. "This has all come up so fast that we've hardly had time to think about details. We'll have to talk about what we're doing for the next few days."

"I'll be staying here with Tyler, of course. I'll take an indefinite leave of absence from work. It's a bad time for the agency, with all the rumors and investigations going on there, but they'll have to manage somehow without me."

Jackson raised an eyebrow. "Are you sure they can?"

Because her work had been such a sore subject between them for so long, Laurel immediately went on the defensive. "Regardless of what you so often imply, I have always put Tyler's needs ahead of my job."

He held up a hand, his expression suddenly weary. "I'm not trying to start anything. I know Children's Connection depends on you, that's all."

"Yes, they do, but Tyler needs me more. I'll call Morgan first thing in the morning to arrange for my leave."

He nodded. "I'll need to check in on the job site a few times during the next few days, but I won't have to spend much time there."

Laurel bit her tongue, but her expression must have revealed more than she had intended. This time it was Jackson whose defenses went up. "I'll be here as much as I need to be, but I can't afford to lose my job now. I'm the one who carries Tyler's health insurance, re-member? Your job isn't going to pay the medical bills, especially with you taking a leave of absence."

Laurel looked down at her lap and shook her head. "I'm not trying to start anything, either. I didn't say any-thing about your work."

"You always make it clear enough that you think I spend too much time working. Even though you know we need the money."

"And you make it just as clear that you've never wanted me to work at all, even if it helps with the money."

His eyes narrowed. "I've never needed help support-ing my family."

It was an old argument, and one Laurel doubted they would ever settle. When it came to family roles, Jack-son's attitudes were straight out of the last century—the *early* part of the last century.

Carl Reiss had taken such pride in the fact that his wife—a hardworking, financially strapped waitress when he'd met her—had never had to work since he'd married her. Jackson had always believed it was his responsibility to provide his son with a full-time mother, like he'd had during his entire childhood.

No matter how often Laurel had tried to explain it to him, he just couldn't seem to grasp the fact that her work gave her something she simply couldn't find within the walls of their nice, middle-class home. And it wasn't money. Yes, she dealt with every working mother's guilt and stress, but she truly felt as though she was a better mother because of her career.

Jackson had never quite understood that Laurel was nothing like Donna Reiss, whose whole life revolved around her husband, son and grandson, and who had never seemed to need anything more. Unfortunately, Laurel and Jackson had been married for several months with a child on the way before that first glow of giddy infatuation had dimmed enough to let them see their differences.

Drawing a deep breath, Laurel reminded herself that a crisis with a child's health could cause stress in even the healthiest marriage. She and Jackson were facing months of difficult times ahead. It would do no one any good, especially their son, if they fell apart now.

"I really don't want to quarrel with you tonight," she said, making no effort to disguise her fear and exhaustion. "I just want to get back to Tyler."

Jackson released a long sigh. "I don't want to quarrel, either. I'm sorry. It's been a…rough day."

Because she understood him well enough to know

what Tyler's illness was doing to him, especially considering Jackson's compulsive need to take care of his family, she felt her irritation with him fading. "Yes, it has. For both of us. And I'm sorry, too."

Their eyes met across the table. For just a moment they were connected again, mentally bonded, the way they had been that first time they had met at a party he hadn't wanted to attend. It was as if they had been able to sense each other's emotions, an ability they seemed to have lost sometime after the birth of their child.

Someone dropped a tray on the other side of the room. The crash made Laurel and Jackson start, breaking the visual contact between them, along with everything else. Laurel reached for her purse while Jackson disposed of their trays.

They didn't say much as they returned to Tyler's room, simply agreeing that Jackson would return early the next morning with a change of clothes for her. He offered to stay the night with her, but she reminded him of how small the room was, adding that someone had to take care of things at home during the next few days.

Tyler was still sleeping when they entered his room, his beloved penguin clutched against his chest. Donna sat in the rocking chair, very close to the bed. Carl paced from his wife's side to the single window and back again.

"Go home, Mom. Get some rest," Jackson urged her. "It's going to be a long week."

Donna reached out to smooth Tyler's hair. "I hate to leave him here."

"Laurel's staying with him."

"Yes, of course." Without looking at Laurel, Donna

bent to brush a kiss over Tyler's flushed cheek. "Good night, precious. Gammy will see you tomorrow."

Jackson ushered his parents out. Donna bade Laurel a polite good night, but it was Carl who stopped in front of her, taking her hands in his work-roughened ones as he searched her face. "You'll be all right?"

"I'll be fine."

"You call if you need anything, you hear? Anything at all."

This was where Jackson had gotten his deeply in-grained sense of responsibility to his family. Just as Carl had been providing for Donna for more than thirty years, he now seemed to feel as though he should offer his protection to his son's wife in a time of crisis.

Donna thrived on being pampered and cosseted, while Laurel was more likely to feel smothered and sti-fled. Still, she couldn't help but respond to the genuine concern in Carl's kindly eyes. "Thank you. I'll let you know if I need anything."

Satisfied with her answer, he released her and turned to follow his wife out of the room. Jackson stayed another hour. Keeping their voices low to avoid disturbing Tyler, he and Laurel continued to discuss the practicalities of the next day—rearranging their work schedules, contacting their insurance agent, canceling a couple of appointments. Both very cordial and efficient, they kept their emo-tions—about their son and each other—tightly reined.

Eventually, Jackson glanced at his watch and sighed. "I might as well head home. You're sure you don't need anything before I go?"

"Just bring back the things on the list I gave you when you come back in the morning. I'm set until then."

He nodded. "Call me if you think of anything else."

"I will." She watched as he stood for a moment beside the bed, looking down at their sleeping child. Jackson reached out a hand as if to stroke Tyler's tousled hair, but then drew it back, perhaps because he didn't want to disturb the boy. He turned away from the bed with visible reluctance.

Laurel stood beside the door as Jackson prepared to leave. Though it was quiet in this room, sounds from the hallway outside drifted in—staff talking and laughing at the nurses' station, carts squeaking on the linoleum, the rhythmic swishing of the janitor's broom. They were sounds she heard often in her job as a placement social worker for the Children's Connection adoption agency, which was affiliated with this hospital, but it was all different tonight. Unnervingly so.

Jackson must have read something in her expression. "You're sure you don't want me to stay?"

Even as she assured him once again that everything would be fine, she wondered how many more times she would have to say it before she believed it herself.

Jackson bent his head to kiss her goodbye. The very slight hesitation just before their lips touched had nothing to do with current circumstances; she had noticed it several times when he'd kissed her during the past few months.

Watching the door close behind him, she couldn't help thinking of the kisses they had shared early in their whirlwind courtship—eager, passionate, joyous and thorough. There had been no hesitation between them then, not even at the very beginning. She couldn't pinpoint exactly when the kisses had changed, or what had caused the change, but she felt the gulf between them growing wider all the time.

Impatiently shaking her head, she turned back to the rocking chair. She had a sick child to worry about now. This was no time to analyze the condition of her ailing marriage.

Thursday was, perhaps, the longest day in Jackson's life. Every minute seemed to crawl past with agonizing slowness. He had never been one to sit still for very long, and the forced inactivity of hospital waiting was a frustrating ordeal for him.

Laurel's attention was focused exclusively on their son, of course. Jackson's mother spent most of the day at the hospital and she, too, dedicated herself to keeping Tyler calm and entertained. Laurel and Donna were, as always, impeccably polite to each other.

Jackson paced, restlessly roaming the room and the hallways, rocking on his feet, trying not to think about the surgery tomorrow and trying not to envy his father, who had decided to spend the day working, since there was nothing productive he could do at the hospital.

It wasn't that he didn't want to spend the day with his family, Jackson assured himself with a touch of guilt. It was just that there was nothing here for him to do. Nothing to make him feel as though he was accomplishing something worthwhile.

He lasted until midday. When it occurred to him that he, Laurel and Donna were all simply sitting there watching Tyler eat his lunch, he surged impatiently to his feet. "I think I'll go see how things are going at the job site."

Tyler immediately set down his spoon and pushed away the rolling bed tray. "I go, too."

Forcing a smile, Jackson ruffled his son's hair. "Not this time, buddy."

The boy's lower lip protruded in a familiar manner. "Don't wanna stay here."

"I'll be back soon. I promise."

But Tyler had had enough of this place. Shaking his head, he held out his arms to his father, looking fully prepared to launch into one of his rare, but daunting, tantrums. "Daddy. Wanna go with Daddy."

Jackson could almost feel Laurel's disapproving look on the back of his neck, silently blaming him for starting this when things had been going so well before. He grew immediately defensive in response, as he so often did with her lately. "There's really nothing I can do here for now," he said to her. "And I have responsibilities to my job."

"As do I," she murmured.

Always the peacemaker, Donna jumped in hastily to avert Tyler's impending outburst and placate his parents. "Tyler, sweetie, Gammy's going to play a game with you as soon as you've finished eating, remember? We talked about it. And, Jackson, there's no reason for you to stay here twiddling your thumbs now when you'll very likely be here all day tomorrow. Run along to take care of things at your job site. Actually, Laurel, you can check in at your office, too, if you'd like. It isn't as if you would be far away. Tyler and I will be just fine here, won't we, darling?"

She spooned a bite of orange sherbet into the boy's mouth as she spoke. That treat, and the promise of a game with his beloved grandmother, was enough to mollify him somewhat. He sniffed and reached again for the spoon.

"I'll stay with my son," Laurel said.

Was that another dig at him? Jackson could no longer tell if he was only imagining disapproval in her eyes when she looked at him. "Guess I'll go on, then. Have fun playing your game with Gammy, Tyler. I'll be back soon and I'll have a surprise for you, okay?"

He heard Laurel sigh, but Tyler smiled. For now Jackson told himself that was enough.

As he left the hospital room, he couldn't help remembering a time when Laurel had smiled at him with such affection. And he wondered sadly whatever had happened to those smiles. He missed them. He missed *her,* damn it.

Stalking through the hospital exit doors, he headed for his truck on the parking deck. He needed to be at work. At least he felt somewhat in control of that part of his life, if nowhere else.

Three

Laurel knew the day was moving too slowly for Jackson, but as far as she was concerned the time was speeding past too quickly. Every hour that went by was another hour closer to the time when her baby went under the surgeon's knife.

She felt as though she was clinging to her sanity by her fingernails. Nervous from the beginning about her ability to be a good mother, especially considering the miserable example set by her own, she didn't know what she was supposed to do now, in this time of crisis. She didn't even know what questions she should be asking of the medical professionals who bustled in and out of Tyler's room during the day.

Lacking a strong role model and reluctant to reveal her maternal insecurities to Jackson or his parents, Laurel had long ago come up with a plan of sorts. Her own mother had been so incompetent in the role, had made so many mistakes, that it seemed obvious that Laurel should ask herself what her mother would do in any situation—and then do the opposite. Since Janice had tended to disappear whenever Laurel needed her most, Laurel had no intention of leaving Tyler's side during this ordeal.

"Are you sure you don't want to take a break, Laurel?" Donna asked late that afternoon. "Except to go with Tyler for his tests this afternoon, you haven't left this room all day. You even ate your lunch in here, what little you choked down. At least I had a chance to get out for an hour when Carl came by for a late lunch with me. Why don't you go out for a walk in the meditation garden? It's lovely out there now that it's stopped raining."

"I'd rather stay with Tyler," Laurel replied, keeping her voice low, as Donna had. Tyler had fallen asleep a short while earlier. Though he was a heavy sleeper, neither of them wanted to risk waking him from his nap too soon, which would leave him cranky for the remainder of the evening.

Donna glanced at the wall clock. "Jackson should be back soon. Maybe you and he can have dinner in the cafeteria."

"Perhaps." Laurel made a show of studying one of the informational brochures a nurse had given her earlier, though she was having trouble concentrating on the guidelines for postoperative care.

"I, um…" Donna cleared her throat delicately, a sign that she wasn't sure how her next words would be received. "I hope you aren't annoyed that Jackson felt the need to work this afternoon. He's so much like my Carl. Neither of them can sit still for long when they could be doing something worthwhile, instead. Carl instilled a strong work ethic in Jackson from a very early age, you know."

"I'm not annoyed." And she didn't need Donna lecturing her about her husband, she thought resentfully. And then she sighed and ran a hand through her dark-blond hair, aware that weariness and stress were making *her* cranky. Maybe she should be the one taking a nap.

"Jackson tries so hard to be like Carl." Donna's eyes were unfocused now, her voice barely louder than a whisper; it almost seemed that she was talking more to herself than to Laurel. "It's almost as if—"

"As if what?"

Donna blinked, then shook her head impatiently. "I suppose I'm just tired."

"Then maybe you're the one who should get out for a while. There's really no reason for you to sit here with me."

Donna's red-tinted lips twisted into a smile. "You probably wish I would leave for a while. But I…well, I just need to be close to my grandson today."

Because that was one sentiment she understood completely—perhaps the only thing she and Donna had in common—Laurel merely nodded and looked down at the brochure again. She really needed to prepare herself for Tyler's postoperative care.

Jackson sat at the same cafeteria table at which he had sat the night before, overlooking the same rapidly darkening courtyard. It was dinnertime again, though a bit earlier than he had eaten the night before. This time it was his parents, rather than his wife, who faced him from the other side of the table.

Despite Jackson's attempts to coax her out of the hospital room, Laurel had insisted on dining from a tray in Tyler's room. He'd gotten the distinct impression that she wanted the rest of them to leave her alone with her son. And he couldn't help resenting that she seemed to be closing him out again.

"We may have to physically restrain her from going into the operating room with Tyler in the morning," he muttered, stabbing his fork into the pasta on his plate.

"She's just worried about him," Donna said soothingly, toying unenthusiastically with her own chef's salad. "She doesn't want to let him out of her sight, as if nothing bad can happen to him as long as she's with him to protect him. I understand completely."

Jackson shrugged. "Wish *I* understood her completely."

There was a taut moment of silence.

"Jackson," Donna said rather tentatively, "you and Laurel are going to need each other during the next few weeks. Don't let this ordeal drive a wedge between you."

Jackson figured his parents had to be aware that his and Laurel's marriage had been shaky for a while now. They weren't stupid, nor were they unobservant, especially where he was concerned. "To be honest, I don't know what, if anything, Laurel will need during these next few weeks. Even if she does need something from me, she sure as hell won't admit it."

It wasn't like him to complain, and he was almost surprised to hear the words escaping him. Apparently the stress of his son's illness was affecting him more than he had realized.

He knew Laurel hadn't been as fortunate as he had when it came to having supportive, always-available parents. Her father had abandoned her early, and her mother had been, from what little Laurel had told him, pretty much worthless as a parent, finally getting killed in a car accident while Laurel was still in high school. But knowing about Laurel's troubled upbringing didn't help him understand her much better, especially since she absolutely refused to open up to him.

"I've been aware that your marriage has been strained lately," Donna admitted with regret. "But I'm sure you can work it out, darling. Laurel loves Tyler so much. As reserved as she is about her feelings, anyone can look at her and see that. And since you love him just as much, that's something the two of you share. Maybe this crisis will draw you closer together, if you'll let it."

Because he thought his mother needed to hear it, Jackson nodded and murmured, "Maybe you're right."

He wasn't so sure himself. Laurel seemed like a stranger to him these days. So different from the laughing, playful, passionate woman he had swept into marriage.

God, he missed that earlier Laurel. He would give anything to understand what had become of her.

And then Carl spoke, typically uncomfortable with the strong emotions surging around him. "Everything's going to be fine."

That simple. And that certain. Carl Reiss would do

anything in his power to keep his family out of harm's way. Unfortunately, when it came to this particular emergency, Carl was powerless. Jackson didn't have the heart to point that out. It was the first time he had been faced so incontrovertibly with the proof that his wise, calm, mechanical-genius father couldn't fix everything.

The remainder of his appetite evaporating, he set his fork down and reached for his water glass.

"You should eat, Jay," Carl said gruffly. "Keep up your strength."

"Yeah. In a minute." He figured it was time to change the subject. "You know what's been bugging me all day?"

"What's that, dear?" Donna inquired.

"The doctor said Tyler's condition is hereditary. That Laurel or I carry a recessive gene that causes it. Yet Laurel insists there's no history of sudden cardiac failure in young males on either side of her family. Though she and her mother were estranged from most of their family, Laurel said she would have known about something like that. Apparently, both of her parents bragged about what strong and healthy families they came from—people who tend to live to ripe old ages. It's ironic, of course, that Laurel's mother was only in her thirties when she died in a car accident."

He watched his parents exchange a quick, grave look.

"Dad, are you sure you don't remember hearing about any young uncles or cousins who died unexpectedly? You lost a younger brother, didn't you? You told me he drowned, but it is possible he suffered heart failure first?"

"My kid brother drowned when the old fishing boat he and his friends were in sank in the middle of a lake," Carl answered without looking up from his food. "Had nothing to do with his heart."

Something in Carl's tone let Jackson know that he found this line of questioning disturbing, perhaps because of the painful memories of his long-lost brother. Jackson regretted bringing that old pain to the surface, but for some reason this question had been nagging at him since the first conversation with Dr. Rutledge. "Okay, so that was an unconnected tragedy. But what about—"

"Really, Jackson, there's nothing to be gained by fretting about this, is there?" Donna's voice sounded unusually sharp. "What does it matter whether you or Laurel carry the gene—unless you're worried that *you* have the condition?"

"I don't," he assured her. He still hadn't confirmed that with his own physician, but he felt confident in that respect. "Still, if I carry the gene—if the Reiss family carries the gene—we should probably let Uncle Bill's boys know about it. They're still in college now, but they'll want to be screened, and they'll want to know about this recessive-gene thing when they have kids of their own."

Donna and Carl looked at each other again, and this time Jackson was puzzled by their expressions. As Jackson watched, Carl reached out to place a hand reassuringly over Donna's. "We'll think about that another time. Let's just concentrate on getting Tyler well, okay?"

There was something there, Jackson thought with a

frown, his intuition ringing warning bells. Something that blanched his mother's face and deepened the fine lines around her eyes and mouth. What the hell?

He decided to let it go for now. "I stopped by the blood bank on the way back from the job site and gave blood, since they said that's a standard request when a family member is having surgery. They won't actually use my blood for Tyler, of course, but having family members donate keeps the blood supplies healthy. Maybe you want to stop by sometime tomorrow, Dad? Have you ever given blood before?"

Jackson had always considered his dad the bravest, strongest man he knew, so it was with some amusement that he watched a bit of the color drain from Carl's tanned, weathered face. "Um, no. I haven't ever gotten around to it."

"It wasn't bad, really. Didn't hurt at all. I'll probably donate again when enough time has passed. I'll get a card in the mail in a couple of weeks that designates me as a donor and tells me my blood type. Funny, I don't even know my blood type. I assume it's the same as yours or Mom's," he added, glancing with a smile at Donna.

His smile faded when he saw her expression. "Mom, are you okay? You've gone as white as a sheet. It's okay, you don't have to give blood if you can't bear the thought of it. It won't affect Tyler."

"I'm—" Donna looked to Carl.

"Your mother's tired," Carl said. "And worried about the surgery tomorrow. Maybe I should take her home to rest."

"Maybe you should." Jackson didn't like seeing his

mother in this condition. She had seemed fine earlier. Maybe it was just all catching up with her.

He felt suddenly guilty for unburdening his problems with his marriage on her at this stressful time. "Take a sleeping pill if you have to tonight, Mom. Get some rest. Everything will be fine tomorrow, just like Dad said."

She nodded and whispered, "Yes, I'm sure it will."

Jackson was startled to see a glimmer of tears in her eyes as she looked away from him. He might have pressed for a better explanation of her distress then, but Carl put an end to the discussion by gathering plates and trays and escorting Donna out of the cafeteria.

Jackson followed with a puzzled frown, wondering what, exactly, had been going on beneath the surface of that odd conversation.

Laurel accidentally overheard a snippet of disturbing dialogue a short while after Jackson and his parents returned to Tyler's room after dinner. Donna and Carl had said they were on their way home as soon as they'd had a chance to kiss Tyler goodnight. While they did so, Laurel slipped out of the room for a few minutes to walk down to the soda machine in the waiting room.

Jackson used to tease her about what he called her addiction to diet soft drinks, she remembered as she fed quarters into the machine and pressed the selection button. He didn't tease her about much of anything anymore.

She had paused at the end of the hallway to open the bottle for a sip of her drink when she heard Carl speaking just around the corner. "Let it go, Donna. You don't know for sure where the gene came from."

"I could call and ask if he knows anything about it." Donna's voice sounded different than Laurel was accustomed to hearing it. High-pitched. Almost scared.

"And what good would that do? Tyler's condition was discovered in time for treatment. That's all that really matters. Jay doesn't have to know."

"He's going to find out, Carl. Don't you see? Somehow during all this testing and discussion, he's going to find out. And I'm not sure what that will do to him. He's already under so much stress, with his relationship with Laurel so strained and Tyler so ill."

The sound of her name roused Laurel out of her temporary paralysis. She had no business listening to this, even if they were talking about her family.

Making sure her heels clattered as she walked, she turned the corner and looked surprised to see Carl and Donna standing there in a quiet alcove, their heads very close together as they talked. Donna's face was ashen and Carl's grave as he held his wife's hands. Both of them started guiltily when they saw Laurel.

"I thought you two were on your way home," she said, hoping her voice sounded natural. "Is anything wrong?"

Donna made a visible effort to pull herself together. "I'm just having a bit of a panic attack, I suppose. Even though I'm confident everything will go well tomorrow, I can't help but dread it a bit."

There was obviously much more to Donna's distress than concern about Tyler's surgery. Knowing this wasn't the time to pursue it, Laurel merely nodded. "I know. I feel the same way."

"I'm taking her home to rest now," Carl said, tucking Donna's arm beneath his and moving toward Laurel. "I hope you manage to get some sleep tonight."

"I'll try."

Carl reached out to rest a work-roughened hand against Laurel's cheek. "You lean on Jay through this, you hear? He's a strong man. He'll take care of you."

Laurel knew Carl was trying to help, but her instinctive response was to assure him that she didn't need anyone to take care of her. She was strong. She'd always had to be. She had learned very early in her life that being strong and self-sufficient earned her the respect and approval of others, while depending on someone else too often led to disappointment and heartbreak.

"Take Donna home," she said rather than directly responding to his words. "She needs to rest."

Both Carl and Donna looked vaguely disappointed by Laurel's evasion, but then, she was used to sensing disapproval in them, she thought as she watched them walk toward the elevators. Still thinking of the words she had overheard, she entered Tyler's room.

Jackson sat in the rocking chair with Tyler on his knee as they watched a cartoon on the television together. Scooby-Doo. Their favorite.

As usual, Tyler clutched the stuffed penguin he called Angus. Jackson had bought him that toy on one of their trips to the Oregon Zoo. Tyler was almost obsessed with the famous Humboldt penguins display there. He never tired of watching the funny little creatures waddling along their rock walkways or torpedoing through the waves and currents of their pool. Whenever Jackson took a rare Saturday afternoon off from work, he and Tyler usually visited the zoo, their special place.

Laurel paused just inside the doorway for a moment, studying them. They looked so much alike. So perfect together.

Emotions roiled inside her as she looked at them. Her feelings for Tyler, at least, were clear-cut. Overwhelming love. Pride. Fear for his future.

It wasn't so easy to define the way she felt about Jackson.

He glanced up when she entered. Though he noted the soft-drink bottle in her hand, he made no comment other than to say, "Your boss called while you were out. He said to call if you need him or Emma for any reason. Said they would be checking on you tomorrow."

"That was thoughtful of him."

Jackson's grunt could have been an agreement, or merely an acknowledgement that she had spoken. They rarely talked about her job, or his either, for that matter, since their work seemed to represent so many of the problems between them.

Laurel settled in the recliner, cradling her soft drink between her hands. "I saw your parents on their way out," she said, choosing her words carefully. "Your mother seemed rather stressed."

"I thought so, too." He glanced at Tyler, whose attention was still focused on the television program. "I guess we can both understand why."

"I suppose." But Donna hadn't been fretting about the surgery. Laurel had gotten the distinct impression that her mother-in-law was worried about something else instead. It had sounded very much as if Donna were keeping a secret from her son—a secret she was terrified Jackson would discover.

Laurel couldn't help speculating about what that secret was, especially since Donna had worried about medical tests bringing it to light. Was Jackson adopted?

And if that were the case, how would Jackson react to the news if he were to find out? Why would Donna and Carl have kept it from him?

Through her job with the adoption agency, Laurel frequently counseled prospective adoptive couples. Her advice was that such information should be provided to the adopted children from an early age. Secrets had a way of coming to the surface, and it was easier for everyone concerned if the truth was known from the start.

Knowing how close Jackson was to his parents, she couldn't begin to predict how he would react if he found out they had kept something like this from him for so long.

Laurel was also disturbed by Donna's comment about the strained state of Jackson's marriage. Had Jackson been talking to his parents about her? The very possibility made her chest tighten.

She stretched out in the recliner, propping her feet up as she took another sip of her drink, then set the capped bottle aside for later. She hadn't slept much the night before, and weariness and stress were catching up with her.

Still mentally replaying Donna's overheard words, she leaned her head back and closed her eyes, letting the sounds of the cartoon and Tyler's giggles wash over her.

Laurel dreamed of the day she met Jackson.

The summer-afternoon party wasn't a typical event

for either of them. The purpose of the gathering was to celebrate the adoption of the homeowners' infant son, and Laurel had been invited as the social worker who had helped arrange the adoption. The new father was a successful businessman who had recently hired the construction company Jackson worked for to build several new stores for him. Jackson, along with several of his management-level co-workers, had been invited to the gathering to welcome their client's son.

Later Laurel would think what a cliché their meeting had been. Eyes meeting across a crowded room. Everyone else fading into a misty background. Her toes curling when he smiled. Sparks of sexual awareness coursing through her when their hands touched.

They had left the party together a short while later. They'd driven to Cannon Beach, where they'd walked barefoot in the sand at sunset, listening to the shorebirds that nested on Haystack Rock. The salty breeze tossed their hair and tugged at their clothes—clothes they had abandoned in a hidden nook among the rocks after sunset. They had been daring and reckless and impetuous that night. By dawn the next morning, they had been in love.

She dreamed of that beach. Of the birds and the rocks and the sand and the stars spread above them like an endless, bright future. She dreamed of conversation and laughter, of passionate whispers and hoarse cries. Of two young people so desperately in love that they had let their emotions sweep them into a life neither of them had been prepared for....

It was his gentle touch on her cheek that woke her.

She opened her eyes to find Jackson's face close to

hers as he knelt beside the recliner. The room was quiet now, the television dark and silent. Tyler lay on the bed, curled around his penguin, sound asleep. Even the clatter from the hallway seemed unusually muted just then.

"How long have I been asleep?" she asked, her voice still husky.

"About an hour. You really went out." His thumb moved against her cheek again. "There are tears on your face. Are you worried about tomorrow?"

Tears? Remembering snatches of her dream, she pushed herself upright and ran a hand through her hair. "I suppose I am."

"It's going to be okay, Laurel. Everything's going to be okay." His tone, combined with the set of his jaw, made it clear he would accept no other possibility.

That obsessive need of his to be in control, to make sure everything in his world turned out exactly the way he wanted it to, was etched all over his face.

As if he had read something of her thoughts in her expression, Jackson gave her a crooked smile. "I sound just like my dad, don't I? Making well-intentioned guarantees I can't back up. Dad's philosophy has always been that nothing bad can happen if he refuses to acknowledge the possibility. I guess he passed some of that trait to me."

His comment reminded her of the conversation she had overheard between Carl and Donna in the hallway earlier. She wondered again how Jackson would react if it turned out that he was adopted. Would Jackson understand, as she had come to see during her years as a social worker, that Carl was no less his father even if it had been love, rather than biology, that had bestowed that title upon him?

Or maybe she had completely misinterpreted what she'd heard. She'd never been a particularly skilled eavesdropper, had never wanted to be. And even if her guess had been right, that was between Jackson and his parents. Now that Tyler had been diagnosed and was being treated, she couldn't see how Jackson's genetic history mattered at the moment.

"You'd probably better head home and try to get some sleep," she told him, changing the subject. "Tomorrow's going to be a trying day and it will start early."

"I thought maybe I'd stay here tonight. I know they only want one parent to stay in the room all night, but there are recliners in the waiting room."

"There's no need for you to do that. You won't be able to sleep well here, and you'll want to be rested tomorrow."

"What makes you think I'll sleep any better at home?" He turned his head to look at the child on the bed. "I can't imagine sleeping a wink tonight."

"Still—"

"Laurel." He frowned, his voice losing the gentle tone with which he had awakened her: "The decision is mine to make."

She locked her hands in her lap. "Of course."

For just a moment the invisible wall between them had lowered. Now it was back. She couldn't for the life of her decide which of them kept rebuilding it—though she suspected it was a joint project.

He covered her hands with one of his, his work-toughened palm pleasantly rough against her softer skin. "Don't close me out of this, Laurel. He's my son. We're a family. We need to be together in this."

After a moment, she turned her hand so that their fingers linked. "I'm not trying to close you out. If it makes you feel better, you should stay. I simply wanted you to get some rest, for your sake."

"I appreciate that, but I need to stay."

"Then stay."

He looked down at their joined hands, his expression grave. "We'll get through this."

She nodded slowly. For now, for Tyler's sake, they would put their differences aside, she promised herself. They would face the problems between them when their son was completely healthy again.

Four

Jackson went home only long enough to shower and change and feed Tyler's goldfish. The house seemed so quiet with no one there but him. To his anxiety-sensitized ears, the few noises he made seemed to echo through cavernous spaces.

Though hardly a mansion, it was a nice house in a safe neighborhood, built for a growing family. Four bedrooms. Two and a half baths. The house also featured a good-sized fenced yard for Tyler to play in, a two-car garage, and a redwood deck Jackson had built himself, with help from his father. Not that he had a lot of spare time to enjoy that deck. He could hardly remember the last time they'd cooked out on the gas grill or dined at the umbrella-shaded wrought-iron table.

Probably Laurel and Tyler ate out there on nice summer evenings, since Tyler usually had his dinner before Jackson got home from work. Jackson was lucky on most days to get home in time to play with the boy for a half or so before bedtime.

He had to pay for this nice home he provided for his family, he thought with a touch of the defensiveness that so often accompanied thoughts of his work. Laurel had told him that she would be satisfied with a more modest house, but he'd wanted his kids to grow up in a good neighborhood. And even though it meant working long, hard hours, he was perfectly able to provide for his family.

He had pictured Laurel staying home to enjoy this nice house with their son and maybe another child or two. That had been before Laurel had changed so drastically, drawing away from him and going back to her social work. He hadn't expected her to return so soon to her job finding homes for other kids, leaving their young son in the care of an expensive nanny.

They'd never gotten around to discussing more children.

Shaking his head impatiently, he glanced down at the sheet of paper in his hand. Laurel had sent him another list of things she needed him to take back to her. The hospital provided showers for parents of hospitalized children, so she would be able to freshen up there. Reading the list, he entered her bedroom and opened the closet door.

Her bedroom. He scowled as he glanced around the impeccably neat room decorated in light woods and cool pastels. It had been over a year since Laurel had moved into what they had originally intended for use as a guest room. Tyler had been going through a spell of having nightmares, and since the master bedroom was downstairs, Laurel had slept up here to be closer to Tyler's room.

Once the nightmares had ended, her excuse for staying in this room had become that Jackson's frequent late hours were disturbing her sleep. It wasn't at all uncommon for him to be in meetings until after ten. He would often arrive home to a dark and quiet house. Much like it was now, he thought with a scowl.

Despite having separate bedrooms, he and Laurel hadn't maintained a strictly platonic relationship. The physical attraction between them had always been strong. Sometimes when he held her after making love with her, he could almost pretend they were happy.

Because they were in for a long day of sitting and waiting at the hospital tomorrow, she had asked him to bring one of the knit jogging-style outfits she liked so much when she wasn't dressed for work. The fitted T-shirts, elastic-waist pants and zippered jackets were comfortable for her and flattering to her slender figure. He chose one in navy with baby-blue piping and a matching baby-blue T-shirt. He'd always liked that color on her. It brought out her clear blue eyes.

Did he tell her often enough that he noticed what she wore? That she always looked beautiful to him? Flowery speech and fulsome compliments didn't come naturally to him, but that hadn't seemed to matter to her during their courtship, when they had never seemed to lack for anything to say. It was only much later that he had realized that in all their carefree chatter, she had shared very little of her deepest thoughts.

He supposed he had shared no more of his own. He had always tried to display his feelings through his actions, not his words. He would say that lack of communication was a definite problem in his marriage.

But that was something they could try to solve later. As he stuffed her clothes into an overnight bag, he told himself they had more urgent matters to worry about now. Once their son was well, there was no reason why he and Laurel shouldn't be able to work out the rest of their problems.

He refused to accept the possibility that either situation might not have a happy ending.

Laurel felt as though she could easily jump right out of her skin. She wanted to pace the hospital room, but she was afraid she would disturb Tyler, who had dropped off rather fretfully only a couple of hours earlier.

With the help of a pediatric social worker, she and Jackson had tried to prepare Tyler for what to expect tomorrow, but Laurel knew the child was still confused and somewhat frightened. As for herself, she was terrified. And no amount of calm, patient counseling from experts could change that.

The door opened and she looked around from her chair, expecting to see one of the nurses popping in for a routine check. Instead, it was Jackson who tiptoed in, his gaze going first to the child in the bed, and then to her. "Can't sleep?"

"No. You, either?"

"No."

"I knew you couldn't sleep out there in those uncomfortable recliners."

He knelt beside her chair. "The recliners are comfortable enough. A couple of other guys are out there snoring away. I just can't close my eyes without thinking about the surgery tomorrow."

She sighed and nodded. "I know that feeling."

"Laurel—" His voice was hardly loud enough for her to hear, certainly not loud enough to carry to Tyler, even if he were awake. "Are you sure we're doing the right thing? How do we know the diagnosis we've been given is even right? Maybe there's nothing wrong with Tyler's heart, after all. Maybe Rutledge misread the tests. Maybe we should take him to a few more doctors before we do something as risky as major surgery."

"The doctors didn't misread the tests. Dr. Rutledge is one of the best in the business. He wouldn't make a mistake like that."

"Everyone makes mistakes."

"Not this time. The whole staff agrees with him."

"Still, how do we know that surgery is the best option at this time? Maybe we should—"

She reached out to lay a hand on his arm, feeling the tension that seemed to vibrate through him. "I understand your panic. Don't you think I'm feeling the same way? But the longer we put this off, the more risk there is to Tyler."

"Just listen, okay? I was talking to Chandra at work today and she told me about this doctor in Seattle—"

"We already have a doctor I trust and respect," Laurel cut in, pulling her hand back into her lap. "I'm not interested in hearing about some doctor in Seattle."

Jackson sighed gustily. "Look, she was just trying to be helpful."

"Well, it isn't helpful." Nor did she appreciate the fact that he had left the hospital today and spent the time he was gone listening to medical advice from his boss's attractive and predatory secretary.

Laurel had known for some time that the brunette and buxom Chandra had her eye on Jackson, and while she didn't think there was anything going on between the two of them, she resented knowing he had been talking about Tyler with the other woman. Of course, she had talked to several of *her* co-workers today, too, but that was different, she assured herself. None of her associates was trying to seduce her away from her spouse.

It wasn't that she was jealous, she told herself. It was just that she hated being talked about behind her back. Having her parental decisions questioned and examined played on her deepest insecurities.

Jackson rose to his feet, irritation mirrored in his movements. "We were just talking. Something you and I don't seem to do much of these days," he added in a mutter.

"And when would we talk?" she retorted. "Since you're at work more than you're home, Chandra and your crews are the only ones who have a chance to talk with you."

His nostrils flared. "Surely we aren't going to have this argument again now."

She pushed both hands through her limp hair. "You're right," she said wearily. "This is absolutely not the time to argue. About anything. We've said that before, but I seem to keep doing it. I'm sorry."

"You're worried," he said, his manner stiff enough to let her know he was still annoyed. "I understand that, but there's no need to take it out on me."

"I've already acknowledged that," she replied, the words clipped.

He started to say something else, but the door opening interrupted him. A young aide slipped into the room, carrying a clipboard. She nodded politely when she saw them at the side of the room.

"Just making my rounds," she said in the hushed voice the staff tended to use during the night shift. "You two better get some sleep. Tomorrow's going to start awfully early. Is there anything I can do to make either of you more comfortable?"

"No, thank you, Tara." Laurel made an effort to smile at the young woman. "We're fine. Just worried about tomorrow."

"That's understandable. But Dr. Rutledge is the best. He saved my sister's baby who was born with a defective heart two years ago."

"That's encouraging to hear," Jackson replied. "Your sister's child recovered completely?"

"Oh, yeah. He's a little pistol now. Right in the middle of the terrible twos." Pausing by the bed, Tara smiled down at Tyler. "Your little boy is precious. All the staff have commented about how sweet and well behaved he is. I know you're both very proud of him."

Laurel and Jackson shared a glance then, reminded of their purpose for being in that place at that time. For Laurel, at least, their argument seemed suddenly trivial and inappropriate. Nothing else really mattered now except getting Tyler well.

Tara moved on to the next room, leaving a taut silence behind her. And then Jackson rested a hand on Laurel's shoulder. "We do have a great kid."

"He looks so much like you," she murmured, looking at the little face on the pillow.

"He has your nose."

"Tilt at the end and all."

Jackson ran a fingertip lightly down the bridge of her nose. "I've always liked that little tilt. On both of you."

The tiny shiver that ran through her was entirely involuntary. Achingly familiar. Whatever their differences, she had always responded quite strongly to Jackson's touch.

His arm tightened slightly around her shoulders, as if he sensed her response to him. In that area, at least, he knew her quite well. "We don't have to be at odds during this, Laurel. We're a team, with one goal. Our son's recovery."

Her throat tight, she nodded.

"I want to be here for you if you need me," he added.

She felt her stomach clench. It was just the sort of comment that always made her edgy. Maybe if Jackson had said that they needed each other... But he would never admit that sort of vulnerability.

"We're both strong people," she said carefully. "We'll get through this."

She was aware that her answer didn't completely satisfy him. "Laurel, if you—"

"Mommy?"

She stepped immediately toward the bed, feeling Jackson's arm fall from her shoulders to his side. "I'm here, sweetie."

Reassured, Tyler snuggled back into the pillow, curling himself around Angus and closing his eyes again.

Jackson waited until it was apparent Tyler was asleep

again before he spoke quietly. "We aren't very good at it, are we?"

Laurel turned with raised eyebrows. "At what?"

"At being a team."

"No, I guess we're not," she whispered. She could almost feel the weight of blame lying heavily on her shoulders. She should have known she wouldn't be any good at this. What in her dysfunctional family history had made her believe she could succeed at being a model wife and mother?

Jackson drew a deep breath, his own expression grim with guilt. Knowing his overdeveloped sense of responsibility, she imagined he was accepting the fault as his own. She watched as his jaw hardened with resolve. "I'm not giving up. We'll keep working at it until we get it right."

No, he wouldn't give up, she thought with a touch of sadness. Admitting defeat wouldn't suit his self-image of the strong and capable head of their household. But shouldn't there be more to a marriage than staying together because they didn't want to admit they had made a mistake?

Had she been allowed, Laurel would have stayed at Tyler's side during the entire operation. Instead, she sat in the surgery waiting room, every nerve ending in her body on anxious alert. A closed Bible sat like a talisman in her lap. Donna had brought it to her that morning, saying the time would pass more quickly for Laurel if she sought comfort in the verses.

Though she was rather touched by the gesture, Laurel had been unable to concentrate long enough even to open the book. Her eyes kept turning to the clock on the opposite wall, watching the hands move so slowly that she constantly fought the urge to check if it was still operational.

Unusually subdued, Donna sat nearby, while Carl and Jackson paced. Other people were grouped in the large area, attended to by a couple of smiling, gray-haired volunteers in bright blue jackets. The volunteers kept the coffee pot refilled, and the aroma of steadily dripping coffee almost, but not quite, masked the antiseptic smell of hospital cleaners.

It was a bit quieter in this surgery waiting room than it had been in the larger waiting room, whether because of the gravity of the procedures underway or because it was still so early in the morning, Laurel couldn't have said.

"Everything okay here, Mrs. Reiss?" one of the sweet-faced volunteers asked as she stopped by Laurel's chair. "Can I get you any more coffee?"

Glancing at the woman's plastic nametag, Laurel shook her head. "No, thank you, Irma."

"Anyone else?" Irma looked at Jackson and his parents as she made the offer. When they, too, declined her assistance, she nodded and moved away, after assuring them that Kathleen O'Hara, their surgery team liaison, would be by soon to give them an update from the operating room.

"Laurel?"

Hearing her name, she turned her head, then rose. "Hello, Morgan."

The tall, dark-haired director of the Children's Connection smiled as he took her hands. Always a pleasant, congenial man, his recent marriage to his beloved

Emma had added a new glow of happiness to his striking blue eyes that no one who knew him well could
miss. Because she knew and liked them both, Laurel
was pleased that Morgan and Emma had found each
other. They seemed to be a strong, united team—something she couldn't help envying a bit.

But his expression now was one of concern for Laurel. "How are you holding up?" he asked.

"I'm doing okay," she said, though she knew it was
usually a waste of time to try to put on a falsely brave
front for this man who was so adept at reading people.

"Any news yet?"

"No. The operation just started about twenty minutes
ago. The surgeon said it could take a couple of hours."

"Is there anything I can do for you? Get for you?"

Attempting a shaky smile, Laurel shook her head.
"But thank you for offering."

He squeezed her hands a bit more tightly, encourag-
ingly. From Morgan, the gesture was almost effusive.
His marriage to the outgoing and demonstrative Emma
was loosening him up a bit, Laurel thought with a brief
ripple of amusement.

"You know where to find me if you need me," he
said.

She nodded. "Thank you, Morgan."

Something made her glance toward her husband, who
was watching them with a frown. Morgan, too, looked
that way, then released Laurel's hands and stepped toward Jackson. The two men had met on several occasions, of course, but the most generous term that could
be used to describe their relationship was cordial. Barely.

And that, Laurel thought, was definitely Jackson's

fault. He hadn't wanted her to return to work in the first place, and he had always blamed Morgan for luring her back, even though she had told him Morgan had nothing to do with her decision.

Whatever Morgan sensed about Jackson's opinion of him, he had always been unfailingly polite, as he was now. Extending his hand, he said, "Hello, Jackson. I just told Laurel to be sure and let me know if there's anything I can do for either of you today."

Jackson nodded. "Thanks. We're doing okay."

"You know that everyone at the Children's Connection has Tyler in their thoughts and prayers today."

"We appreciate that." Jackson moved closer to Laurel as he spoke, not so subtly positioning himself between his wife and her director.

Morgan spoke briefly with Donna and Carl after Laurel introduced them. He left a few minutes later with the promise that he would check in again to see if they needed anything.

"Your boss seems like a very nice man," Donna said to Laurel a few moments after Morgan left.

"Yes, he is." Laurel took her seat again and locked her hands in her lap. Now that her momentary distraction was over, her concentration returned to the distant operating room.

It was like flipping a switch, Jackson thought with an irritably bemused shake of his head as he studied his wife from across the surgery waiting room.

Nearly an hour after Morgan Davis had stopped by, Laurel was visiting with another of her professional associates, philanthropist Leslie Logan. And, just as she had earlier with Morgan, Laurel had gone from being tense and silent and withdrawn to animated and talkative. Still visibly anxious about the surgery, but more willing to share what she was thinking and feeling. She even allowed Leslie to hug her and give her the maternal sort of comfort she wouldn't have accepted so willingly from her mother-in-law.

The wife of a wealthy and wildly successful entrepreneur, Leslie Logan dedicated many hours—and dollars—to the Children's Connection adoption foundation she had supported almost from its inception. Jackson figured she had to be around sixty, but she was an attractive woman with her slender build, reddish-gold hair and lively brown eyes.

He knew Laurel had always admired Leslie, to the point that he'd once accused her of hero-worshipping the older woman. Sure, Leslie had worked tirelessly on behalf of the foundation in addition to raising a houseful of kids, both biological and adopted. And she had carried on bravely after losing her first child to a kidnapper several decades ago, even though she still had to be haunted by the memory of that loss.

Jackson could understand why Laurel admired the woman. But if Laurel was so impressed with that sort of wealth and influence, why had she married a construction foreman who would probably never move in those circles?

So maybe he had a bit of a chip on his shoulder when it came to Laurel's wealthy associates. He figured that was natural enough when a man measured his accomplishments by how well he provided for his family. Yeah, sure, he and Laurel had met at a fancy society party, but he'd never tried to pretend to her that he was one of the upper crust, or even particularly aspired to being one. A hard worker who made a good living— that was how he saw himself.

He'd never taken a dime he hadn't earned himself, unlike the rich kids who'd inherited their wealth. He'd worked his way up from hammer-swinger to job fore- man and he aspired to someday own a small construc- tion firm that would turn a tidy, if modest, profit. A nice house, an occasional family vacation, a decent educa- tion for his kids—that had been enough to satisfy his parents, and it was all he asked for himself.

He'd thought at the beginning that Laurel felt the same way. She'd never asked for more, though, of course, Lau- rel never asked for anything. But when she had chosen to return to work rather than devoting herself to the full-time responsibilities of motherhood, he'd had to assume there was something missing in their life. And since her only explanation had been vague statements about needing to feel "fulfilled," he still didn't know what the hell she found in her work that he couldn't provide for her at home.

He also couldn't understand why she allowed herself to look so vulnerable in front of Leslie Logan when she refused to show any weaknesses at all in front of her own husband and in-laws. Sometimes it seemed almost as if there were three Laurels—the friendly, outgoing, witty social worker most people knew; the loving, de- voted, infinitely patient mother to Tyler; and the quiet, self-conscious, defensive outsider in the Reiss family. With him, she was a combination of all those Laurels, but there was still a part of herself she kept hidden even from him.

He wondered if any of her friends from work ever saw a glimpse of that hidden Laurel. He found himself wanting very badly to be the one she smiled at the way she had smiled at Morgan and Leslie. Maybe it was his fault that she didn't, his failure to make her feel as valued as they obviously did.

Leslie gave Laurel one final hug, then made her way out of the waiting room. Acting on impulse, Jackson moved immediately across the room to join his wife. "You holding up okay?" he asked her.

She gave a little sigh and pushed a strand of hair away from her pale face. "Barely."

It was a more candid response than he had expected. He slipped an arm around her shoulders. "We should be hearing something any minute."

She nodded against his shoulder. "I hope so."

"I'll be glad when this is all over and Tyler's back home again."

Her reply was heartfelt. "So will I."

"We'll take him to see the penguins as soon as the doctor says it's okay."

"He'll like that."

"Yeah. And we'll all go this time. All three of us."

She nodded again.

He put his hands on her shoulders. "We could have lost Tyler without ever knowing anything was wrong. But we've been blessed with a second chance, Laurel. With Tyler and with each other. Let's try to do it a little better this time, okay?"

There was a soft shimmer of tears in her eyes when she gazed up at him. The sight of them was so rare, and so unexpected, that he felt his chest tighten. Ignoring everyone else in the room, he brushed his lips lightly across hers.

"We'll get through this," he murmured. And for perhaps the first time since he'd been told about his son's illness, he began to believe it.

"Mr. and Mrs. Reiss?" Irma, the volunteer, looked as though she were hesitant to interrupt them.

Without releasing Laurel, Jackson looked around. He felt Laurel clinging to him a bit more tightly as he asked, "Is there news?"

"Your son is out of surgery. He came through just fine. The doctor will be out to speak with you soon."

Laurel seemed to sag just a little. Jackson tightened his hold on her. "When can we see Tyler?"

"Tyler will be taken to PICU, where you'll be able to see him as soon as he's settled in."

"Thank you, Irma."

The older woman smiled and moved on to the next family waiting for news of a loved one.

"I'd better tell Mom the operation's over," Jackson murmured, glancing across the room to where his parents sat anxiously watching him.

"Yes. Your mother doesn't seem to be handling the stress very well."

Jackson had noticed that, himself though he was rather surprised that Laurel had. Donna had been acting downright oddly for the last couple of days, in Jackson's opinion. He'd never seen his mother so jittery and introspective. But then, she'd never faced open-heart surgery for her utterly adored grandchild before either, he told himself. "Let's go talk to her."

Laurel held back a bit. "You go ahead."

He kept a light grasp on her arm. "I thought we were going to work on this team thing," he reminded her.

After only a momentary hesitation, she nodded. "All right. We'll talk to them together."

Satisfied with whatever small victories he could get, Jackson led her toward his parents.

Five

Laurel had thought the time had passed slowly while Tyler was in surgery, but it seemed to creep by even more sluggishly afterward. She and Jackson had already met briefly with the surgeon, who had assured them again that Tyler had come through the operation very well before he'd somewhat apologetically rushed away to his next patient. Kathleen O'Hara had promised to let Laurel and Jackson know the minute they would be allowed into the ICU to see Tyler. And now it was a matter of waiting again.

Carl and Jackson talked Donna and Laurel into accompanying them to the cafeteria for an early lunch. Laurel wasn't hungry, and didn't particularly want to leave the waiting room, but Jackson convinced her in whispers that his mother needed the break. Because even Laurel was starting to be concerned by Donna's visible distress, she reluctantly assented. Maybe it would make the time pass a bit more quickly, she reasoned without much optimism.

Leaving word where they could be found, they took the elevator down to the cafeteria. Carl and Jackson ate hungrily, neither having eaten much breakfast, but both Laurel and Donna only picked at their food.

Donna jumped every time someone spoke to her. Laurel watched her mother-in-law surreptitiously, wondering what, exactly, was going through the other woman's mind. She couldn't help remembering the puzzling snatches of conversation she'd overheard between Donna and Carl, and it seemed obvious to Laurel that Donna was still obsessing about whatever had been bothering her then.

Whatever the problem, Laurel hoped it wouldn't be too upsetting for Jackson when he found out—and she didn't doubt that he would find out, given the way Donna was acting, all but advertising that there was something she was trying to hide.

For the first time in quite a while, Laurel was feeling a bit better about the state of her marriage. Maybe Tyler's illness would forge a stronger bond between her and Jackson than they'd had before, a new level of trust and communication. He seemed to be trying for now anyway, and she was willing to give it another shot, for Tyler's sake, if for no other reason.

It would be just the way their luck went if Jackson's mother did something, even unconsciously, to put a new wedge between them.

A tall man with salt-and-pepper hair and a shorter

woman with brown hair and a sleeping toddler in her arms stopped beside their table. Both of them smiled at Laurel. "Laurel, it's good to see you," the woman said. "How are you?"

"I'm fine, thank you." Laurel gave them a cordial nod as she made a quick mental search for their names. Oh, right. Anne and Bob Hulsizer. And the child's name was… "How is Gregory?" she asked, nodding toward the little boy.

Both parents beamed. "He's wonderful," Anne said, lightly patting the sleeping boy's back. "Worn out at the moment, but he's usually running a mile a minute. It keeps us young chasing after him."

"He's the greatest kid in the world," Bob boasted without a hint of self-consciousness. "Anne and I will never be able to thank you enough for helping us adopt him, Laurel. We just can't tell you how much he has enriched our lives."

"I'm sure Gregory feels very fortunate to have you as his parents," Laurel replied. Then, because she didn't want to seem rude, she quickly introduced Anne and Bob to her husband and in-laws.

Anne looked at Laurel's companions as she explained eagerly, "Several adoption agencies turned us down because of our age, but Laurel really went to bat for us when we signed up with Children's Connection two years ago. She knew how desperately we wanted a child and she knew we would be good parents, so she was willing to fight for us. Fortunately, Gregory was available, and since he was a special child with visual impairments, there weren't a lot of people willing to take him."

"Their loss," Bob added. "He's smart and funny and loving, all of which more than make up for his poor eyesight. Thanks to Laurel, we're the lucky ones who'll get to watch him grow up and develop his full potential."

Laurel was beginning to be a bit embarrassed by the Hulsizers' gushing, though she was glad they were so happy with their special child. "I'm glad everything is working out for you all."

Bob grinned. "Even better than expected. We've just left his doctor's office. Gregory is scheduled for an operation that should prevent him from losing any more of his sight and may even restore some of his peripheral vision. It's a new procedure that's been showing extremely positive results."

"That's very good news," Jackson said. "Congratulations."

Laurel saw no need to mention Tyler's ordeal at the moment, and apparently Jackson didn't, either. The couple moved on, leaving silence at the table behind them.

"You should eat a little more, honey." Carl placed his hand over Donna's. She hadn't spoken at all to the Hulsizers, which, Laurel thought, was yet another indication that Donna wasn't herself. Usually she would have been the first to ask a dozen questions about Gregory and to congratulate them on their positive medical news.

Donna gave Carl a wan smile. "I'm just not hungry."

"Tyler's okay, Mom. You'll get to see for yourself in a little while," Jackson promised.

"I'll feel much better then," she said.

Laurel wasn't so sure. She was certain that there was more to Donna's behavior than worry about Tyler's condition.

As though she sensed that her uncharacteristic pre-occupation was drawing attention, Donna made an ef-fort to contribute to the conversation. "I know Beverly's looking forward to seeing Tyler, too. She made me promise to call her as soon as he's allowed visitors out-side the family."

Laurel had always been uncomfortable with the way Donna had bonded with Tyler's nanny. Donna often stopped by their house to see Tyler while Laurel was working, and apparently she and Beverly spent those visits drinking coffee and chatting.

Laurel had tried not to be so paranoid as to think that those chats ever revolved around her fitness as a mother. She honestly doubted that the nanny would be so un-professional or her mother-in-law so disloyal. But it still bugged her sometimes.

"I'll call her myself, once we've seen Tyler and have an update on his condition," she murmured.

"Oh, I'll take care of that for you. You know what good friends Bev and I have become."

Donna's artless comment made Laurel's frown deepen. Surely Donna hadn't intentionally implied that she had developed no such friendship with her daughter-in-law.

"Laurel has a good relationship with Beverly, as well," Jackson murmured, perhaps picking up on his wife's sensitivity.

"Oh, yes, Beverly gets along well with everyone. But of course, she and I have spent more time together since poor Laurel works so hard. I can't tell you how much I admire your choice of a nanny, Laurel. Since you have to spend so much time away from Tyler, it was wise of you to choose someone so capable to watch over him, even though I know Beverly's services are rather expensive. And her nursing experience will certainly come in handy during his post-surgery care, after you return to work."

Maybe Donna wasn't being so innocently offensive, after all, Laurel thought as her fingers tightened in her lap beneath the table. She found it a bit hard to believe that some of those digs hadn't been deliberate. "I won't return to work until Tyler has fully recovered. I told Morgan that I was taking an indefinite leave of absence to take care of my son."

"Tyler's needs come first with Laurel, Mom. You know that." Jackson's tone sounded rather chiding, which was a rarity from him when it came to his mother.

"I know that," she muttered, though Laurel wondered how anyone could possibly believe her tone was sincere.

Carl spoke quickly. "Can I get you any more tea, Donna? How about you, Laurel? Is there anything else you would like?"

"No." She pushed her chair back from the table and rose. "Thank you, but I'd like to get back upstairs now."

Jackson followed suit. "Yeah. Me, too."

Donna started to rise, but Carl stopped her by placing a hand on her arm. "We'll be up in a minute," he said. "I'd like just one more cup of coffee first."

Donna seemed about to speak, but a look from her husband made her bite her lip and sit quietly instead, as Jackson and Laurel walked away.

"You always accuse me of imagining that your mother disapproves of me," Laurel couldn't help saying as soon as she and Jackson were alone in the elevator going up to the surgery waiting room. "Are you going to tell me she wasn't making a few digs at me just then?"

His first instinct was obviously to defend his mother. But even as he started to speak, he fell silent and shook his head. "I don't know what's going on with Mom today," he admitted. "She did seem to be taking her anxiety out on you, and that wasn't fair. I apologize if she hurt your feelings."

"Why would *you* apologize?" That was just the sort of thing that annoyed Laurel. "You don't control what your mother says or does. And at least you defended me this time."

"This time? Implying that I don't usually—" He stopped and drew a deep breath. "Never mind."

She supposed he was trying to stick to their agreement not to quarrel today, and she reminded herself that she should do the same. Just as Jackson shouldn't have to apologize for his mother's behavior, he shouldn't have to take the blame, either.

"I'm not trying to imply anything," she told him quietly. "Just…thank you for standing up for me."

"We're a team, remember?"

Laurel couldn't help wondering which team he would choose if Donna's newly revealed hostility toward her daughter-in-law escalated into real competition.

Seeing Tyler for the first time after surgery was difficult for all of them. Laurel had to lock her knees to keep from sagging against Jackson at the first sight of her baby with needles in his arms and a plastic tube down his throat.

Jackson made a rough sound low in his chest. Donna gasped, then burst into tears. Laurel tried to be annoyed at her mother-in-law's melodramatic reaction, but she was trying too hard to hold back the tears herself.

The PICU staff had been lenient in allowing all four of them to enter Tyler's unit, and they permitted them to stay for a short while, but then they insisted that only two could remain. Space was limited, and the staff needed plenty of room to monitor and care for their patient.

Carl convinced Donna to let him take her home to rest, leaving Jackson and Laurel to sit by their son's bed. Donna made them promise to call if there was any change at all in the child's condition. She didn't look at Laurel as she left, and Laurel wondered if she had done anything that day to offend her mother-in-law. If so, it had been unintentional. But she had more important things to worry about now, she told herself with a slight shrug.

Putting Donna and her problems out of her mind, she sat quietly in a chair beside Tyler's bed, studying the numbers on the monitors and watching the heavily sedated child's chest rise and fall in the steady rhythm of the ventilator.

Jackson sat in a chair next to Laurel's, on the other side of the room from most of the equipment the staff needed easy access to. They sat without speaking for quite a while, both lost in their own thoughts, their eyes rarely leaving the bed or the monitors. They responded when anyone spoke to them, but neither initiated conversation.

Jackson finally seemed to rouse from his reverie. He glanced at Laurel. "He looks pretty good, don't you think? Considering, I mean. His color's good. Numbers look positive, from what I can tell on those monitors."

He needed reassurance, and Laurel gave it to him, though she thought *good* was a poor choice of an adjective for the way their son looked at the moment. "He's doing fine," she said. "As soon as they can take him off this ventilator, I'm sure we'll see a big improvement."

"Just as well they're keeping him sedated now, I guess. He'd be afraid if he woke up and couldn't speak or pull that thing out of his throat. And I'm sure there's going to be pain, even when they do bring him out of sedation."

"Some pain, of course," she agreed, trying to sound as calm as Jackson about the next steps. "But he'll be given as much medication as he needs to control it."

"We'll make sure of that."

Since neither Jackson nor Laurel were exactly the passive type when it came to their son's medical care, neither of them accepting everything the medical professionals said or did without question, she didn't doubt that Tyler would get the best care they could obtain for him. She was much more concerned with the time after they took him home from the hospital, when his care would be up to her. She still felt so much guilt that she had missed the early signs of his disability. What if she missed something else?

After another period of silence—at least, as quiet as a hospital unit filled with swooshing, beeping and whirring equipment could be—Jackson spoke again. "You know that couple we saw downstairs in the cafeteria? The ones who adopted the kid with the vision disabilities?"

"You mean the Hulsizers?"

"Yeah. They sure think the world of you."

"They're nice people. I like them, too."

"That was a good thing you did for them, helping them find their son. They looked like good parents for him, a happy family."

Though she was a little surprised by his topic, she nodded. "They're very good parents. I knew they would be when I met them and spent some time with them."

"They made it sound as if they wouldn't have gotten a kid at all if you hadn't fought for them."

"Their case was a little tricky," she admitted. "I can't give the details, of course, but there were some problems in their application that made them seem less than ideal on paper."

"But you were able to see beyond the paperwork problems to tell that they would be good parents."

"Yes. Lots of people have made mistakes in their past. That doesn't mean they don't deserve to have children, especially if they can show evidence that they've overcome their problems."

"It's gotta be hard to make calls like that, though. We both know there are people who shouldn't be parents, regardless of whether they look good on paper."

Laurel thought of her own parents—the father who hadn't wanted responsibility, the mother whose only thoughts were of her own fun and pleasures. No, they should never have brought a child into the world. Nor should any social worker ever have approved them had they applied for adoption. But mistakes were made on both sides, and sometimes children were placed in homes that were less than ideal, just as some good potential parents were never given an opportunity to prove their worth.

It wasn't a fair world. But Laurel had made an effort to pair children who had been denied families with couples who had been unable to conceive. Maybe it was a foolish desire to make up for her own unsatisfactory upbringing. Or maybe it was just something she was good at, which gave her a feeling of fulfillment.

It had been a long time since she and Jackson had talked about her work, other than to quarrel about her hours. Of course, the same was true in reverse, she thought with a touch of guilt. She rarely asked about his job either, being more likely to criticize the amount of time he put into it than to show any real interest.

"I just do my best and hope I don't make any drastic mistakes," she said.

And then she turned the conversation to him instead. If they were going to do a better job of communicating, it would have to be a two-way effort. "How are things going at your job site? Are you still waiting on that big delivery from Seattle that's been holding you up?"

Both his eyebrows rose. "I didn't know you were even aware of that."

"I pay attention to your concerns," she said, trying not to sound overly defensive. "I know you deal with a lot of responsibility in your job. Just because I think you could spend less time at the sites and a bit more at home doesn't mean I don't respect what you do."

He started to speak, and she sensed that he was going

to take exception to what she'd said, making her regret her wording. Maybe it had sounded as if she were trying to start another quarrel about working hours, but she really hadn't been.

Instead, he surprised her by saying, "You're probably right. I guess I have spent too many hours at work. During Tyler's surgery this morning, I was thinking of all the evenings I wasn't there to play with him or read to him or tuck him in. I thought it was my responsibility to provide him with the best material things I could afford, but when I thought of losing him, it wasn't the money that mattered. It was the time we could have spent together."

Caught completely off-guard, she blinked at him.

He shook his head, looking somewhat embarrassed that he'd opened up even that much. "Never mind."

She wasn't sure what to say, except, "You're a good father, Jackson. No one doubts that you love Tyler. But maybe it will be good for both of you if you can spend a little more time with him in the future. He doesn't need all those material things, you know. He needs his daddy."

"And his mommy," Jackson replied. "Maybe we can both spend a little more time with him in the future."

Because they had already agreed that spending more time together was one way to put their marriage back on track, Laurel nodded. She was needed at Children's Connection, but she was needed more at home.

Tyler's illness had served as a wake-up call for both of his parents.

Laurel had no complaints about the level of care Tyler received in the pediatric intensive-care unit. His condition was constantly monitored by medical staff who seemed genuinely concerned about his well-being. Laurel and Jackson were made to feel welcome in the unit and were encouraged to ask questions about everything that was done to their son.

Jackson hadn't completely forgotten his earlier worries about medical mistakes. "Do you know that medical error is cited in some sources as the fourth leading cause of death in this country?" he asked Laurel, looking up from a news magazine he had been reading to pass the time. "Adverse reactions to drugs, accidental overdoses, mix-ups in prescriptions between patients—"

"Jackson," she interrupted firmly, "calm down. Those are valid concerns, of course, but you and I are watching everything that's being done with Tyler. We won't be leaving him here alone, but I trust this staff. I work around this hospital every day. I hear who are the good doctors and the ones who have more questionable reputations, and we've got the best. As for the rest of the staff, this hospital administration has spent a lot of money and energy during the past year working on reducing the patient-error rate to the lowest it has been in more than a decade."

"Everyone has seemed pretty efficient," he acknowledged. "But that doesn't mean I'm not going to keep an eye on them for the rest of the time Tyler's here," he added, returning to the alarming article he'd been reading so closely.

Not that her husband was a control freak or anything, Laurel thought with a slight sigh, but she supposed when it came to Tyler's welfare, there was no such thing as being too vigilant.

Just this once she could even be grateful for Jackson's insistence on perfection.

"Mr. Reiss?" A petite nurse's aide poked her curly red head into the unit. "You have a couple of visitors in the waiting room. They said they work with you. They told me it was okay if you aren't in the mood for company, but they just wanted you to know they're here."

Jackson looked questioningly at Laurel.

"Go," she told him. "They made the effort to stop by, it's the least you can do to thank them."

"Come with me. Tyler will be okay for a few minutes."

"Of course he will," the aide agreed. "Actually, it's time for me to take some readings, so both of you should have a little break."

Laurel wasn't enthusiastic about visiting with virtual strangers during that little break, but she didn't want to seem churlish. As she had pointed out, it was thoughtful of Jackson's co-workers to stop by. If he wanted her to thank them with him, she supposed it wouldn't hurt to do so. After all, she reminded herself wryly, she and Jackson had agreed to work harder at being a team.

She didn't like leaving Tyler alone in the ICU even for a short time. She almost changed her mind at the door, but Jackson took her arm and led her out. "We'll be right back," he promised her.

It wasn't overly reassuring to be towed out of the unit by the man who had just warned her about every bad thing that could happen in a hospital.

Six

Jackson had to swallow a groan when he saw who was waiting for him. He'd expected to find a couple of guys from his crew, most likely Joe and Luke, his two best friends from work. Joe and Luke were there, all right, but they weren't alone. Chandra Shoemaker, the boss's secretary, had come along for the visit.

Feeling Laurel stiffen the moment she caught sight of the visitors, Jackson didn't have to guess which one had set her back up. Laurel had never liked Chandra.

The two women had met only a few times, at the annual company picnics and Christmas parties, which were the few events Laurel had attended. She usually used work or Tyler as an excuse not to go with him to his social functions.

Though she had never put her feelings into so

many words, he suspected that she thought Chandra had something going for him. Okay, maybe she wouldn't have been completely wrong. Chandra was a compulsive flirt, and he doubted that she was all talk when it came to her conquests. He wasn't oblivious to the fact that she would have been available to him had he chosen to take her up on her half-teasing advances.

Heck, maybe he'd even flirted a little in return. After all, a man's ego needed an occasional boost, and he sure as hell didn't get that from Laurel. But cheat on his wife? No. That wasn't the way he had been raised.

A real man honored his commitments, Carl had said too many times to count, and Jackson had made a commitment to be a faithful husband. If Laurel didn't understand what that meant to him, well, then, he really was a stranger to her.

"Hey, guys," he said with a falsely bright smile, giving another slight tug on Laurel's arm to move her forward. "Nice of you all to come by."

"How's your boy?" Joe asked with genuine concern on his weathered face. "He doing okay?"

"He's still sedated, but everything looks promising so far." Jackson pushed a hand through his hair. "We're hoping they get him breathing on his own in the next few hours so they can take him off the ventilator."

"This must have been a rough day for the two of you." Shy Luke glanced quickly at Laurel before turning his dark eyes back to Jackson's face. "Anything we can do for you?"

"No, but thank you for offering."

Chandra stepped forward to take Jackson's hand.

"Are you sure there's nothing we can do? We're here for you if you need anything at all, you know."

He patted her hand, then quickly released it, moving subtly closer to Laurel at the same time. "We're doing okay, aren't we, Laurel?"

"Yes, we're fine." Her voice warmed just a bit when she added to the men, "But we really do appreciate you stopping by to offer your support."

Luke flushed a little, as he always did when he felt self-conscious. Joe cleared his throat. "Thing is, we have a little something for the two of you."

He held out a slightly crumpled white envelope. "Some of the guys at work took up a collection for you. We've all had family members in the hospital at one time or another and we know how expensive it can be. You know, eating in the cafeteria and paying for parking and all. Maybe this will help a little."

Jackson's pride cringed at the thought of taking the offering, but he knew it would hurt his co-workers if he refused. How many times had he dug in his pocket for a contribution to something just like this? It had always made him feel good to help out his friends when he could. He supposed the others felt the same way.

"That's really nice of you guys," he said awkwardly. "And women," he added with a glance at Chandra. There were women on the crews, of course. It was just habit to refer to everyone as "the guys."

"It was very kind," Laurel agreed, her warm smile making Joe's flush deepen. "Please thank everyone for us."

Joe shrugged, looking pleased with their response to the gift, as though he hadn't been quite sure how Jackson would react. "Just try not to spend it all on cafeteria food. As good as the food here is, that stuff gets old fast."

"Don't I know it." Eager to put the awkward moment behind them, Jackson stuffed the envelope in his back pocket. "So how'd everything go at the site today? Did that shipment ever come in?"

"I'll let you stay and talk shop with your friends," Laurel said before anyone could answer. "I really should get back to Tyler now."

"You should try to get some rest, Laurel," Chandra said. "You look really tired."

Laurel's smile glittered just a bit. "I'll do my best."

Taking her leave of the men, she turned and left the waiting room, her steps unhurried, her head held high.

Jackson sighed, wondering if he was in for another chilly session with his wife. Was it his fault that Chandra had a catty streak that showed up even when she was making an effort to be nice?

Laurel would probably figure that it was, he thought glumly, and then turned his attention back to his visitors.

She wasn't jealous, Laurel assured herself again back in her chair in Tyler's unit. So what if Chandra was younger, perkier and bustier? So what if she had a habit of looking at Jackson as if he were some sort of exotic, forbidden dessert? Jackson wasn't weak enough nor foolish enough to be taken in by that sort of thing. And besides, he was too honorable even to consider breaking his marriage vows, something his staunchly moral father would have flatly condemned.

Still, Laurel would have liked to be sure that Jackson's fidelity had more to do with his devotion to his wife than to his desire to live up to his father's high standards.

One of the monitors connected to her son began to emit a high-pitched beep, making Laurel jump and half rise out of her chair. Before she could call a nurse, someone was there.

The nurse pushed a button to mute the alarm, then swiftly and efficiently changed an empty IV bag. Murmuring something reassuring to Laurel, she checked Tyler's breathing and readings, then left the unit just as Jackson came back in.

"Is there a problem?"

Laurel shook her head. "One of the IV bags had to be changed. Everything else seemed okay."

"Have they said anything more about taking him off the respirator?"

"No one's mentioned it yet. I guess they're waiting for a doctor to check in."

Jackson frowned and glanced at his watch. "If we don't hear something soon, I'm going to start asking questions until I get answers."

She eyed his face, then glanced down at her lap, saying gruffly, "Maybe you'd like to wipe the lipstick off your face before you start throwing your weight around. People tend to take you more seriously when you aren't smeared with Kiss Me Crimson."

Though she wasn't looking at him, she suspected he flushed a little when he reached up to swipe at his cheek with the back of his hand. "Chandra gave me a kiss on the cheek on her way out. One of those meaningless social kisses people toss around so easily these days. She'd have done the same to you if you'd hung around."

"Not if she wanted to keep her lips," Laurel muttered beneath her breath.

"What was that?"

"Nothing."

"Laurel, you can't seriously believe—"

She stood abruptly. "I think Tyler just frowned. Do you think he's in pain?"

"I think you're changing the subject." But Jackson also stood and moved to Tyler's bedside, studying the boy closely. After a moment, he said, "I don't believe he's feeling any pain, at least not consciously. He's too deeply sedated."

She wanted so badly to gather her baby into her arms and rock him, but she couldn't, of course. Not with all the tubes and needles and monitors stuck in him and on him. She contented herself with stroking his hair. Maybe he sensed her touch; the slight frown she had noticed earlier faded, leaving his little forehead smooth again.

"He seems to know you're here," Jackson murmured, unconsciously echoing her thought.

"I hope so."

"You're a good mother, Laurel."

She bit her lip to the point of pain as all her maternal insecurities flooded through her again. Would a good mother have missed the signs that her son was sick? Wouldn't a good mother have been content to stay at home with her child rather than going back to work even when they didn't really need the money she earned?

Was Jackson only mouthing words he didn't truly believe?

"I do my best" was all she could say.

But standing here now, looking at her unconscious son, she couldn't help wondering if her best was good enough.

Tyler's breathing tube was removed that evening. Because of potential complications of intubation, the doctors wanted the child breathing on his own as soon as possible, a sentiment with which Laurel heartily concurred. She was glad it hadn't been necessary for him to remain on the machine overnight.

Jackson and Laurel were asked to leave for a while to allow the medical professionals room to work, and were assured that they would be allowed back in as soon as Tyler was settled again. She hadn't been out of the hospital in days, so Laurel allowed Jackson to persuade her to go for a walk in the meditation garden.

It had rained that afternoon, as it so often did in Portland, but the rain had stopped for a while, leaving the air cool and slightly damp against her cheeks. Her jogging suit was warm enough, but just barely, the breeze seeping through the knit fabric. Her gray tennis shoes squeaked a little in the shallow pools of water left on the narrow walkways.

Bordered by the walls of the hospital wings, the garden was quiet, almost empty this late on a Friday afternoon. A few smokers gathered around an ash can in a nook specified for that purpose at the far end of the garden, but they were far enough away that Laurel could almost feel as if she and Jackson were the only ones around, if she ignored the diners in the cafeteria on the other side of the glass wall.

She breathed deeply of the rain-washed air, realizing for the first time how cooped up she'd been during the past few days. Even when working, she spent little time in her office, since she often visited prospective adoptive parents in their homes. She hadn't read a newspaper or watched television since Tyler was hospitalized, so she had no idea if there were any important events going on in the world. But, then, nothing else really mattered to her now except her child's health.

Because she and Jackson had spent the day in Tyler's unit, she hadn't met any of the other family members currently sitting vigil in the hospital, but she was no more in the mood for socializing than she was for current events briefings. She just wanted to go home—and she wanted to take Tyler with her.

"Mom said Beverly stopped by again this afternoon. She's eager to see Tyler," Jackson said after they had walked in silence for several minutes.

"Surely she knows that only family members are allowed in ICU."

"I think they'd let her come in for a few minutes tomorrow if we say it's okay."

Laurel hesitated, then shook her head. "I know she's fond of Tyler and I really am very grateful to her for noticing the signs of his illness. But does it sound much too selfish of me to say that I wish she would wait a little while before visiting again? I'd rather just keep it family for now."

"So would I," he admitted. "Beverly's a nice woman,

but I've always seen her as an employee, not a member of our family."

And not an employee he had wanted to hire, she added silently. To Jackson, Beverly had always represented the biggest source of conflict between them—Laurel's decision to return to work.

"I've taken an indefinite leave of absence from work," Laurel reminded him. "I'll be with Tyler during his full recovery. Since we can't afford to pay Beverly while I'm on leave, she'll probably need to look for another position. When he's well again and I feel comfortable about returning to work, we can talk about rehiring her if she's available, or someone else if she's not."

Jackson paused to study a small bush that was drooping beneath the weight of the raindrops that still clung to its early-spring leaves. "So you think you will want to return to work soon?"

"Right now, I can't think of anything except getting Tyler well," she said candidly. "But I don't want to close any doors for the future, either."

Jackson didn't say anything in response to that, though she suspected there were plenty of things he would have liked to have said.

A large fountain stood in the very center of the garden. Water cascaded six feet down tiers of stone, splashing merrily against the smooth river rocks at the base. Later in the summer, mounds of flowers would add color to the greenery planted around the fountain. Laurel paused to listen to the falling water, realizing as she did so that the spot where she and Jackson stood now was blocked from the view of both the diners and the smokers, offering a little area of seclusion in this place where privacy was in short supply.

As if deliberately changing the subject, Jackson said, "Mom and Dad will probably be back soon. Sure wish I knew what's going on with Mom. Whether it's just the stress of Tyler's surgery or something more."

"I'm sure she'll tell you if there's anything bothering her. You and your mother have always been able to talk." Too much so, if they'd been talking about her, Laurel would have liked to add.

"Yeah, I guess. So, what are you going to do tonight?" he asked, abruptly changing the topic again. "They won't let you sleep in Tyler's room, will they?"

"No, not in ICU, although they said we could go in to see him whenever we like. I suppose I'll sleep in the ICU waiting room with the other parents. What about you?"

"Yeah, I'll stay, too. Actually, you could go on home and get some rest. I'll call you if—"

"No." She shook her head forcefully to emphasize the refusal. "I want to stay. Especially tonight. He might need me."

Jackson didn't push it, probably because he knew it wouldn't have made any difference. Laurel would sleep in the waiting room, reluctantly, but she had no intention of leaving the hospital tonight.

A cool, damp breeze teased the hair on the back of her neck that had escaped the loose ponytail she'd worn for convenience. Her resulting shiver made Jackson wrap his right arm around her shoulders. "Getting too cool?"

"A little. Maybe we should go back in. They could have Tyler ready for us by now."

Jackson glanced at his watch. "The nurse said we should give them half an hour. It's only been fifteen minutes."

"Maybe they'll finish early."

"Let's wait just another couple of minutes."

She heard him draw a deep breath, and she knew it was even harder for him to be cooped up indoors all day than it was for her. Especially when there was so little he could do to make himself feel useful. "Maybe you should go home tonight. Get some sleep."

"No. Not tonight. I want to be here in case— Well, I just want to be here tonight."

In case anything bad happened. He didn't have to finish the sentence for her to understand what he meant. Both of them knew that the first twenty-four hours after surgery were the most critical in the recovery process. Although they had been repeatedly assured that Tyler's recuperation was progressing as expected, they had been warned of all the potential, if unlikely, things that could go wrong.

"Nothing bad's going to happen," she said aloud, feeling almost as if she had to keep reiterating the affirmation to make it come true.

Jackson tightened his arms around her shoulders and brushed his lips against her forehead. "We won't let it," he murmured.

She leaned against him. Maybe if they focused together on the same compelling wish—Tyler's complete recovery—it would come true, she thought somewhat fancifully. They were a team, he kept reminding her. They were stronger together than apart. At least, that was what she wanted to believe.

Taking advantage of the seclusion of the nook in which they stood, the deepening shadows, the seductive music of the falling water, Jackson moved his lips from her forehead to her cheek. And then to her mouth.

He'd kissed her so many times and in so many ways during their four years together. She had thought she knew every nuance of his kisses. Yet this one was different in some way she couldn't quite define. It was almost as if, for the first time since she'd met him, Jackson wasn't quite so sure of himself. As if his inability to protect Tyler from this crisis had shaken his confidence in every way.

She reacted instinctively. Putting her arms around his waist and tilting her head back to return the kiss, she offered comfort and reassurance, even as she sought the same things in his embrace.

Being held by Jackson was always a heady experience. His body was toned from years of hard work, his shoulders broad, his arms roped with muscle, his thighs long and solid. He was the very model of virile masculinity. On the night they had met, she had been swept off her feet by all that overwhelming maleness. She still was at times, even when she was equally tempted to strangle him for it.

He ended the kiss very slowly. For just a moment he rested his forehead against hers, as if clinging to the closeness. And then he sighed. "I suppose we'd better go back in."

Did his tone mean that he was as reluctant as Laurel to return to the realities waiting inside the hospital?

For the brief time they'd been out here in the garden, shielded from view of the hospital, they could almost pretend everything was fine. But now it was time to go back in.

Swallowing a sigh, she dropped her arms and stepped away from him.

There were eight other children in the pediatric ICU that night—fewer than usual, Laurel was told by one of the nurses. Other families huddled in the ICU waiting room's chairs and recliners.

When she entered just before 10:00 p.m., Laurel noted that several families had made little nests for themselves, their chairs surrounded by bags of snacks, books, magazines and craft materials to help them pass the long hours of waiting. She found out very quickly that the parents who had been there longest had claimed certain sections of the room as their own.

There was no television in this room, though she was informed that a TV lounge was located just down the hall. This room was for resting, waiting, visiting quietly with family and friends. During the nights, it became a place for exhausted parents to sleep as best they could. At ten, the lights were dimmed, blankets and pillows were distributed and all but two visitors per patient were asked to leave.

There were other facilities available for the families of hospitalized children. A Ronald McDonald House was located not far from the hospital, providing sleeping and recreation quarters for people who lived too far to commute easily to visit their children. Most of the people settling into the waiting room for the night either lived nearby or simply refused to leave the hospital while their children were there. Laurel could have gone home, of course, but she simply couldn't bear the thought of being a full half hour away if Tyler needed her for any reason.

"Here you go, honey. These two recliners are free tonight." A pleasantly homely woman who looked to be in her late forties patted the arm of a chair next to her as she spoke to Laurel. "Mr. and Mrs. Carson's boy was moved to a regular room this afternoon."

"Lucky them," Laurel said, sinking into the recliner closest to the woman while Jackson took the one beside her.

"Yes. Their boy was in a bad car accident with his grandparents. Both of them were killed, I'm sad to say. It was touch and go for young Daryl for a while there, but he's on his way to a full recovery, praise be."

Laurel set the blanket and pillow she had been given to one side of her chair. "That is good news."

The older woman nodded. "We get to know each other in here after a while. All of us start to care about the other patients. My name is Carol Grissom, by the way. My fourteen-year-old daughter's in unit 4. She was hurt riding her bike day before yesterday. I told her always to wear her helmet, but she didn't listen that day."

The woman stopped for a hard swallow, and then she added with forced cheerfulness, "She has a head injury, but the doctors tell me she's showing signs of improvement. I'm sure she recognized my voice this evening, even if she couldn't respond yet."

Brought out of her own anxiety for the moment, Laurel touched the woman's hand. "I hope everything goes well for her."

"Thank you, dear. It's been a tough time for me. I'm a single mother—Patty's dad died several years ago—and my only family is a brother who lives in San Francisco. Patty's all I have."

How lonely it must be for this woman to have to go through this ordeal alone, Laurel thought with a wave of compassion. It made her grateful to have Jackson's support, grateful even for his parents, whom she knew would do anything she asked of them during Tyler's crisis.

She felt vaguely guilty for not recognizing how much luckier she was than other people. At least Tyler's chances of recovery were excellent, barring unforeseen complications. That was more assurance than many of these worried parents had to cling to.

"I'm Laurel Reiss. And this is my husband, Jackson. If there's anything we can do for you—"

"Isn't that sweet of you." The woman cut in with a faint smile, looking genuinely touched by the offer. "I know you have troubles of your own. You have the little boy who had the heart surgery this morning, don't you?"

"Why, yes. His name is Tyler."

"You look a little surprised that I know about him. There hasn't been much to do to keep me distracted except to find out about everyone else," Carol admitted candidly. "I've spent as much time with Patty as they would allow, but when I'm not in there with her, I'd go crazy if I didn't have something to do to take my mind off her condition."

"I don't blame you." Laurel made a mental note to have one of her friends on the hospital's social worker staff check in on Carol, if no one had done so yet.

A couple in the far corner of the room knelt beside their chairs for what appeared to be a quiet prayer before sleep. Carol lowered her voice as she leaned closer to Laurel. "Robert and Jean Wyzinski," she murmured, nodding toward the praying couple. "Their little boy has very little chance of surviving, but they haven't given up hope. They can't, I guess."

"What's wrong with him?" Laurel asked in a whisper, feeling sympathy gather in a lump in her throat.

"He had routine surgery to correct a minor problem with his stomach and he developed a post-surgery infection that has turned into encephalitis. He isn't responding to any antibiotics and his condition keeps getting worse instead of better. He's been in a coma for the last three days. They've been told to expect the worse, but they cling to their faith."

"How—" Laurel swallowed hard, her sympathy now touched with fear of something similar happening to Tyler. "How old is their son?"

"He's eight. Their only son, though they have two older daughters. I feel so sorry for them."

Carol was obviously a people person, someone who cared about others as intensely as she was curious about them. Laurel already liked her, but she didn't have the energy for further conversation about other people's problems for now. She was so very tired.

With a faintly apologetic smile, she reached for her blanket as someone dimmed the lights in the room. "I think I'll try to get about an hour's sleep before I look in on Tyler again."

Unoffended, Carol glanced at her watch. "The nurse has promised to come get me at midnight to sit with

Patty for a while. I suppose I'd better get some rest, too. Good night, Laurel."

"Good night, Carol." Laurel settled back into her recliner, turning her body toward Jackson as she did so. He was already stretched out, his eyes closed, though she knew he wasn't yet asleep.

As if to confirm that thought, he reached out to her. She placed her hand in his and let her eyelids drift closed. Just before she fell into a restless sleep, she offered a prayer of hope—for her child, and for all the others whose loved ones waited and worried.

Seven

Laurel nearly jumped out of the big recliner less than two hours later when someone touched her. It felt as though she'd just managed to doze off when she opened her eyes to find a young nurse's aide leaning over her.

"Mrs. Reiss? I'm sorry if I startled you." The young woman spoke in a whisper.

Laurel tried to be as considerate, though fear made her voice rise a bit. "What's wrong? Is it Tyler?"

"Nothing's wrong. He's just restless and we thought he might like to hear your voice. You asked us to come get you when he woke up."

Proving he hadn't been sleeping deeply either, Jackson lowered the footrest of his recliner. "He's awake?"

"Not completely. We still have him lightly sedated."

Laurel was already on her feet. Since she'd slept in

her jogging suit and sneakers, she was prepared on that short notice to follow the nurse. "We can both come?" she asked, noting that Jackson was sliding his feet into his shoes.

"Of course."

They left the waiting room as quietly as possible to keep from disturbing the few people who actually seemed to be sleeping. Laurel noted that Carol's chair was empty, so she figured she must have been summoned to her daughter's unit.

As the nurse had explained, Tyler wasn't fully awake, but had surfaced from the heavy sedation enough to whimper softly and squirm a bit in the bed. He quieted when either of his parents spoke soothingly to him, so Laurel and Jackson spent the rest of the night taking turns sitting with him and taking catnaps in the waiting room. Neither got much sleep, and both were exhausted by the time Donna and Carl arrived Saturday morning.

Laurel noted immediately that Donna seemed calmer, even if her behavior was still not quite normal. Something was obviously bothering her, but maybe she had decided to keep whatever it was to herself until Tyler was better.

Carl seemed even more protective of his wife than usual, but other than that, Laurel could detect few real changes in his demeanor. Maybe he was a bit more awkward with Jackson than usual? Maybe he didn't quite meet his son's eyes when he spoke to him? Or was that simply her sleep-deprived imagination at work?

Tyler was somewhat more responsive that morning, though still heavily medicated for pain. He even managed a smile for his grandmother, which brought a new film of tears to Donna's eyes. Laurel couldn't bring herself to mind that the smile wasn't for her, because it obviously meant so much to her mother-in-law. And almost immediately afterward, Tyler groggily asked for his mommy. Laurel kissed his forehead and stroked his hair until he went back to sleep.

"You and Jackson both look so tired," Donna said a short while later. "Why don't you try to get some sleep while Carl and I sit with Tyler?"

"No, I'm fine," Laurel answered instantly.

"Yeah, me, too," Jackson said, not to be outdone.

Donna didn't try to push the issue.

Laurel wondered if she had been a bit too optimistic when she tried to stand a few minutes later and had to discreetly hold onto the back of a chair until the world stopped spinning. Okay, so she was tired, she conceded. But she wouldn't give it to the weariness now, not as long as Tyler needed her.

Confident that she was strong enough to get through this, she went out to the coffeemaker that was always freshly filled, and poured herself an extra-large cup of the strong brew.

The Wyzinski child took a turn for the better that afternoon. Another severely injured boy didn't make it. Laurel found herself celebrating for the one family and grieving for the other, their situations made more personal to her because of her own child's ordeal.

When she wasn't sitting with Tyler, Laurel chatted with Carol Grissom. Unfortunately there was no change in Patty's condition, but Carol continued to distract herself from her worry by monitoring all the other patients and their families. She asked several times about Tyler and seemed genuinely pleased when Laurel reported that he was improving steadily.

Laurel certainly couldn't complain about Tyler's care. The doctors and surgeons, nurses, aides and other staff were all professional and efficient. She heard a few muttered complaints from other families, but honestly had none herself. Kathleen O'Hara still checked in with her at least once a day to make sure there were no problems with Tyler's care, but Laurel had nothing but praise for the hospital staff.

She couldn't help wondering if her association with Children's Connection, which shared board members with the hospital, had something to do with the level of service her family received. She hoped that wasn't the case, but for Tyler's sake, she would take any advantage she had.

Several of her co-workers stopped by during the day to see if there was anything they could do to help. None of them stayed long. Because of her unexpected absence, the caseload for the other social workers was increased. In addition to that, there had been several other troubling problems in the agency lately—an attempted kidnapping of one of the babies slated for adoption, a rumored mix-up in the sperm bank of the fertility clinic, a few whispers of involvement with illegal baby trafficking. Even the potential of scandal connected with the foundation was enough to have the board of directors and all the staff on full alert.

Since Laurel was the type to focus intently on her own cases and tended to hurry home to her son as soon as her work was finished, she knew little about the rumors or gossip—only enough to worry her, too.

Children's Connection performed such a valuable service to childless couples and children in need of homes. Laurel was proud of her association with them, and she refused to believe there was a darker side to the foundation. She tended to agree with some of the other employees that someone was deliberately trying to smear the reputation of Children's Connection—perhaps someone who had been legitimately turned down as an adoptive parent.

But she couldn't worry about work issues now, she reminded herself as she rubbed her aching head Saturday evening. She had to concentrate on her child, her family. Even Jackson hadn't mentioned his business all day, though she suspected concerns about his job had crossed his mind more than a few times.

"Laurel, are you sure you're okay? You're looking pretty pale."

She dropped her hand from her temple and straightened her shoulders. "I'm fine," she told her mother-in-law, who was sitting in Tyler's room with her while Carl and Jackson took a break to walk outside. "What about you? You've been here all day. Shouldn't you go home and get some rest?"

"I'll leave in a little while." Donna kept her eyes on Tyler's face. The child was sleeping again, as he had most of the day, a result of the medications being pumped through his IV. "He's doing well, isn't he?"

"Yes. The doctor said he's recovering nicely. In a couple of weeks, he'll be running and playing again."

"He'll have to be careful not to overdo it."

"I've been given detailed instructions about his recuperation."

"Maybe you should have Beverly stay with you and Tyler for a few weeks after he gets out of the hospital. Just a suggestion, of course."

"Donna, I don't need a nanny if I'm going to stay with Tyler full-time—which I will during his recuperation."

"Yes, but she's a trained nurse's aide. She was the one who noticed Tyler's health problems in the first place, you know."

Laurel felt the muscles at the back of her neck tense. "Yes, so you've pointed out. Repeatedly."

Donna flushed. "I'm not criticizing you, of course. I'm sure if you had been with him as much as Beverly, you would have seen the signs yourself."

That comment, of course, only made matters worse as far as Laurel was concerned. "I spend a great deal of time with my son, Donna. I work thirty to thirty-five hours a week. Certainly not that much compared to most working parents. And not nearly as many hours as Jackson works, though I don't hear you attacking him for not knowing Tyler had a congenital heart condition."

"I wasn't attacking you, Laurel. And Jackson works hard because he has a family to support. It's his responsibility as a husband and father."

"And my responsibility as a wife and mother is to devote myself entirely to their needs, completely sacrificing my own? Honestly, Donna, what century are you living in?"

Donna started to snap back an answer, but she

stopped herself with a visible effort, taking a deep, un-steady breath and holding up her right hand. "We're both tired. And worried. This isn't the time to talk about the differences between us. I'm hardly in a position to criticize anyone else's mothering skills. God knows I've made a mess of things myself."

"You? The perfect mother?" Laurel couldn't resist saying.

Donna made a sound that seemed to be a cross be-tween a bitter laugh and a choked sob. "Hardly."

Obviously, this strange conversation had something to do with whatever had been bothering Donna for the past couple of days. Maybe Donna's uncharacteristi-cally open criticism of Laurel had more to do with her own insecurities than any ill-feelings toward her daugh-ter-in-law. And maybe Laurel should try to reach out to see if there was anything she could do to make things better between them. But as Donna's hurtful remarks echoed in her aching head, she bit her lip and remained quiet, instead.

Jackson and Carl came back into the unit soon af-terward. Laurel thought again about how the hospital had relaxed the ICU rules, allowing families and pa-tients themselves to become more actively involved in their care. As far as Laurel was concerned, it was a change for the better. She wouldn't have been at all co-operative had anyone tried to keep her away from Tyler.

By Sunday morning, Jackson was becoming al-most as worried about Laurel as he was his son. She was pale and drawn, with purple shadows beneath her eyes and a fine tremor in her hands. She hadn't had a full night's sleep, or a solid meal for that matter, since Tyler had been diagnosed Wednesday afternoon. The ICU waiting room was no place for a good night's rest.

He would be relieved when Tyler was moved back into a regular room with a spare bed. The doctor had told them that move could come as early as Monday, and that there was a good possibility Tyler could be home by the following Monday.

When his parents showed up at noon, both still looking a bit more grim than usual, but obviously rested, he drew Laurel aside. "You have got to get some sleep before you collapse. And how many of those antacids have you popped today? You need food—real food, not the quickest thing the cafeteria serves."

He watched as Laurel dropped the hand with which she had been rubbing her forehead, an obvious indication of a headache. She'd been rubbing that same spot on and off ever since Wednesday. "I'm—"

"You're not fine," he interrupted before she could finish her stock reply. "You're wiped out. Let me take you home for a few hours while Mom and Dad are here to sit with Tyler."

Her face took on that mulish expression he recognized all too well. "No, I—"

"Laurel." Jackson placed both his hands on her shoulders and looked directly into her eyes, ignoring the few other people sitting in the ICU waiting room. "Tyler is recovering even more quickly than the doctors expected. He enjoys being with my parents. He's still sleeping most of the time, anyway. He'll be okay without you for a couple of hours. You have to get some rest or you aren't going to be in any shape to take care of him when he goes home next week."

Her chin rose. "I can take care of my son."

"I have every confidence in that. But you have to take care of yourself, too. Let me take you home to rest."

She didn't want to. Her reluctance to leave the hospital while Tyler was here was evident in every line of her posture. But maybe he had gotten through to her, at least a little, with his reminder that she would have to be in top condition to take care of a recuperating preschooler. "Well…"

"Great. Let's go tell Mom and Dad we're going. You know they'll be perfectly happy to stay with Tyler for a while."

"I can't believe your dad is spending so much time here at the hospital," Laurel murmured, allowing Jackson to practically tow her along behind him. "He's usually too restless and too worried about spending time away from his shop."

"I know," Jackson admitted. "I think whatever it is that's going on with Mom has Dad worried, too. He's barely let her out of his sight for the past couple of days, and the way he hovers around her, you'd think *she* was the one who's sick."

Stopping suddenly, he looked at Laurel with a frown and a clutch in his chest. "You don't think that's it, do you? That Mom's sick and she doesn't want to tell us because of Tyler?"

She gave his question a moment's thought, then shook her head. "I don't think that's the problem. It's just a hunch, of course, but I think something else is bothering her. I'm sure she'll tell you when she's ready."

Hoping she was right, he headed for the ICU again with Laurel close at his side.

It felt so strange entering her house, as if she had been gone much longer than the few days that had passed since Tyler's diagnosis. Even though Jackson had been home every day to check on things and pick up fresh clothing, the house had a hollow, boarded-up feeling for Laurel. She figured it had to be because Tyler wasn't there—and because she had left a part of herself at the hospital with him.

Her in-laws had been predictably happy to stay with Tyler. They had both asserted that they were worried about Laurel's lack of sleep, and wanted to do whatever they could to help her. Familiar paranoia made Laurel suspect that Donna was actually happy to see her leave, giving her total access to Tyler without Laurel hovering nearby.

It was that ignoble thought, as much as the other signs of mental and physical exhaustion, that cemented Laurel's decision to take a short break from the hospital. As Jackson had pointed out, she would be of no use to Tyler if she turned into a sleep-deprived wreck.

Moving in an almost robotic haze, she threw a load of clothes in the washer. She was watering a few houseplants when Jackson, who had been checking phone messages and feeding Tyler's goldfish, caught up with her. "You're swaying on your feet. Come on. You're going to bed."

Taking her hand, he led her to the master bedroom, rather than the room she usually slept in to be closer to Tyler. She was too tired to argue about where she would nap, and it didn't really matter, anyway.

Kicking off her shoes and removing her hoodie, she sat on the right side of the king-sized bed. She briefly considered putting on a sleep shirt, but she was just too weary to make the effort. Raising a hand to the stiff muscles at the back of her neck, she rolled her shoulders in a futile attempt to ease the tension.

Jackson sat beside her. "Neck hurt?"

She dropped her hand. "Kind of stiff, from sleeping in chairs, I guess."

Placing his right hand on her neck, he gave a light squeeze. "Your muscles are tied in knots."

She arched reflexively into his gentle kneading. "Yes, I…mmm."

His left hand joined the right. "Feel good?"

Her eyes were already closed. "Very."

Rotating his thumbs against a particularly sore spot, he drew a sigh from her. "Lie down and I'll give you one of my world-famous neck rubs."

She hesitated for maybe a heartbeat before she swung her legs onto the bed and rolled onto her tummy. Jackson's neck rubs might not have been literally "world-famous," but he did have a special talent. She could hardly remember the last time she'd been on the receiving end. It had been quite a while since she and Jackson had spent any time alone together.

A friend of Donna's who worked in a travel agency had once suggested to Laurel, in front of Donna, that Laurel and Jackson should take a week-long cruise. A second honeymoon.

"It would be good for you both," the woman had added. "Give you a chance to get away from work and routine and spend some time enjoying each other's company. I'm sure Donna and Carl would be delighted to watch Tyler."

Laurel had politely brushed off the idea, saying it wasn't a good time financially or work-wise for her and Jackson to take a week off.

"Besides," she had murmured, "I really don't want to leave Tyler for that long while he's still so young."

Donna had seemed to approve of Laurel's response. "While I would be delighted to keep my grandson, I don't think Tyler would be at all happy to be left behind for a week. I remember how Jackson clung to me at that age. I never left him for more than one night the whole time he was growing up, and then only for emergencies in my family. When I had to leave, Carl was always there for him."

Laurel would be with her child even now if she hadn't been coerced into leaving the hospital, she reminded herself when she began to feel guilty about being at home. And she would spend the night close to him, only a few steps away if he wanted her.

If he did need her during the night, she had to be rested and alert, so she forced herself to relax the muscles between her shoulders. She tried to concentrate on the pleasant massage rather than on her impatience to be back at the hospital with Tyler.

"That's better," Jackson approved. "Let it all go for now."

She sank more deeply into the pillows, deliberately letting her mind empty. She fell asleep with his hands still coaxing the knots out of her neck and shoulders.

She had been asleep maybe half an hour when she woke with a sharp gasp. Though the details were already escaping her, she knew she'd had a bad dream involving Tyler.

She'd heard him calling her, sobbing her name, but she hadn't been able to reach him. She had known it was critical that she get to him, that he was in terrible trouble, but some force had held her back.

And there had been another voice—had it been Jackson's mother's or her own?—telling her she should have known she didn't know how to be a good mother.

She really should have known.

Eight

Jackson had just drifted off to sleep when Laurel's strangled cry woke him. Hearing her gasp Tyler's name, he knew she must have had a bad dream.

"Laurel?" His voice sounded groggy to his own ears as he rose to his elbow. "You okay?"

"I need to go back to the hospital."

He caught her before she could climb out of the bed. "You haven't rested long enough. Try to get a little more sleep."

Her eyes were still unfocused, her movements jerky and uncoordinated. "I can't. I need to get back to Tyler."

"Laurel. Honey, you've had a bad dream. You're still not fully awake. Tyler's fine. Mom and Dad are with him. You're just so tired you're loopy. Lie back down, okay?"

She blinked, staring at him as if bringing his face slowly into focus. "I—"

"A bad dream," he repeated firmly. "That's all it was. Tyler's okay."

Sinking back into the pillows, she looked embarrassed as she turned her flushed face away from him. "I'm sorry I woke you. You need to rest, too."

"I'm okay. Do you need me to get you anything? A glass of water, maybe?"

She shook her head.

"How about something to help you sleep? We have some of those over-the-counter sleeping pills that are supposed to relax you."

"No. I don't want to sleep too long."

He pulled her onto his shoulder and brushed a kiss across her forehead, wishing she wouldn't stiffen up when he held her these days. "Just once," he murmured, "I wish you would let me take care of you. I wish you could trust me enough to believe that you can let go for a little while and the world won't fall apart."

"I never implied that you were untrustworthy," she mumbled in protest. "Not in any way."

"Then trust me now. Trust my parents. Believe that everything will be fine while we sleep because they're capable of watching over Tyler. If we're needed, they won't hesitate to call us immediately."

Maybe his words got through to her that time. Or more likely, he thought with a silent sigh, she was simply too worn out to fight him anymore. Whatever the reason, she closed her eyes and went out again, her body going limp against him.

He, on the other hand, was wide awake now. He lay

there for a long time, holding her and wishing the physical closeness they shared now was more than just illusion.

The next time Laurel awoke, it was a more gradual easing into consciousness. She became aware first that she felt more rested than she had in days. Her muscles had unknotted and her head wasn't aching. And then she realized that she was still cradled in her husband's arms.

She opened her eyes, blinking away the blurriness of deep sleep. Jackson lay on his back with his eyes closed, his left arm beneath her, his right hand resting on his chest. He had removed his shirt, leaving him clad only in loose jeans for his nap.

She lay very still, watching his tanned chest rise and fall with his even breathing. A light rain fell outside, and the watery light slanting in through the bedroom window cast intriguing shadows over Jackson's strongly carved features. She couldn't deny the pleasure she took in watching him sleep. He was such a good-looking man.

She allowed her gaze to drift downward, pausing at the pulsing hollow in his throat, sliding down to the broad, lightly furred expanse between his nipples, traveling even lower to his flat, solid stomach. She spent a moment admiring the way his soft denim jeans hugged his lower half, cradling his unmistakable masculinity and making his legs look a mile long.

When she raised her eyes again, his were open.

"Hey." His voice was still gravelly, a warm groan that elicited a shiver of response in her.

"Hey."

He studied her face. "Your eyes are brighter. There's more color in your cheeks. You must have slept well this time."

"I did." She glanced at the bedside clock, realizing that she'd slept solidly for just over two hours. "Surprisingly so."

"Want to talk about the bad dream you had earlier?"

Embarrassed by the reminder, she shook her head. "I've already forgotten most of it."

She remembered the key points, of course. Tyler's disconsolate cries. Her own frantic, but futile, efforts to reach him. That haunting voice that questioned Laurel's competence as a mother, preying on her deepest insecurities.

"You don't have nightmares very often. At least, not that you've mentioned."

"No. Not since childhood, really."

"You had a lot of nightmares when you were younger?"

They hadn't talked much about her childhood—her choice, mostly, since so many of her early memories were unhappy ones. She'd never wanted to compare their upbringings too closely, since Jackson's had seemed so idyllic in contrast to hers. The one thing she had never wanted from her husband was pity.

But maybe it was time she shared a bit more with him, so he could understand her a bit better. Past time, actually. She deliberately kept her tone light as she answered his question. "I went through a stage of having them almost every night. I guess that's why I identified so strongly with Tyler when he went through that phase last year, even though I was older when mine started. Fortunately, his didn't last long."

"Did your mother sleep close to you when you had nightmares? Did she comfort you the way you did Tyler?"

Here was the tricky part. Still unwilling to draw on his sympathy, she chose her words carefully. "You've heard me say enough about her to know better than that. My mother told me that big, strong girls didn't need anyone to reassure them after a nightmare. Good, smart girls told themselves it was just a bad dream and went back to sleep without disturbing anyone else."

Watching her face a bit too closely, he grimaced. "You told me you pretty much raised yourself. That your mother was gone a lot."

"My mother left me home alone by the time I was six years old. I was already making my own meals and doing my own laundry, putting myself in bed and getting myself off to school in the mornings. She was usually too tired from partying the night before to get up that early. My father was in and out of my life until I was ten or eleven, when he took off for the final time."

She paused, thinking again of Donna's boast that she had never left her son alone. "Our mothers were very different."

"Mine might have been a bit *too* involved in my life at times," Jackson murmured. If he felt pity at the description of Laurel's youth, he kept it to himself. Probably because he knew her well enough to know how much she would dislike it.

She had never heard him say anything that close to a criticism of his mother's child-rearing techniques. There had been times when she'd wondered if he had ever felt smothered by Donna's somewhat obsessive mothering, but she'd never quite had the courage to ask. It had been such a sensitive topic for them from the beginning.

She liked to think she had split the difference between their mothers—maintaining her own life through her job, yet making sure Tyler had the very best care she could provide during the hours she was separated from him.

"It's no surprise we turned out so differently," she murmured. "I wonder why it took us so long to realize that."

"Maybe because we were too blinded by lust?" he suggested, a hint of teasing in his voice as he moved his hand slowly down her bare arm beneath the short sleeve of her T-shirt.

She shivered. "That's entirely possible."

Shifting his weight, he rose on one elbow to lean over her. He rested the fingertips of his free hand against her jaw. "Just because we're different doesn't mean we can't still be good together. Maybe we've let those differences push us apart in the past, instead of using them to make us stronger together."

The words sounded good, Laurel mused, but she wasn't entirely sure anything had really changed between them. They had come closer together during their son's medical crisis, but would it really last when their lives returned to normal? Despite what he had said about celebrating their differences, almost since their honeymoon had ended she had felt as though Jackson was subtly trying to mold her into someone more like his mother.

Perhaps it was an unconscious effort on his part, but

she had always sensed that he wanted her to be different in some way. More dependent on him. More content to stay home while he went out and did his providing-for-the-family routine.

"And now you've drifted away from me."

She focused on his face again. "I was just thinking that we should get back to the hospital soon."

Visibly unsatisfied with her response, he gazed down at her. "We have a little while yet. I told Dad we'd be back by six and it's only four-twenty now."

She started to roll to the edge of the bed. "I'll put the clothes in the dryer while we shower and have a bite to eat. They should be dry by the time we're ready to leave."

"Wait." Cupping her cheek in his hand, he lowered his mouth to kiss her. His lips moved firmly against hers, and the tip of his tongue slipped between her lips.

Considering everything, her immediate response was rather surprising. She would have thought she'd have been too worried and impatient to get back to the hospital to be sidetracked by a kiss. Apparently, she'd have been wrong.

Maybe it was because she so desperately needed a distraction that she found herself wrapping her arms around his neck and kissing him back. Heat radiated from his bare chest through her thin shirt, a warmth that seemed to soak through her skin and swirl inside her abdomen. She shifted restlessly beneath him, her hands sliding hungrily down his back.

Jackson made a guttural sound and gathered her more tightly against him. It was instantly obvious that she wasn't the only one who had become so quickly and intensely aroused. Apparently, they both needed a temporary escape from reality.

They made love silently, fluidly, quickly. They didn't bother with foreplay, since they were both so ready. They didn't waste time fumbling around, since they knew each other so well in this respect. They achieved their satisfaction almost simultaneously.

Just for a moment, they clung to each other, reluctant to end the closeness. Laurel wanted very badly to believe Jackson's assurances that things were getting better between them. But she knew their problems were still there, not resolved, perhaps not even fully identified yet.

Even as the warmth faded, she felt anxiety creeping back in, an urgency to return to the hospital and to Tyler. Either Jackson felt her start to stiffen or he was having similar feelings, because he didn't try to detain her when she rolled away from him.

"Go on and shower," he told her. "I'll put the clothes in the dryer."

"Thank you." She hesitated briefly, feeling as if there were something she should say, but nothing came to her. Gathering fresh clothing into her arms, she turned and walked into the bathroom, closing the door behind her.

To everyone's relief, Tyler was moved into a regular room Monday afternoon. He was already more alert, only lightly medicated for discomfort, feeling just well enough to be fussy. Laurel stayed busy reading to him, watching videos with him, anything she could think of to keep him entertained.

The other parents still in the ICU waiting room

seemed almost as pleased as Laurel that Tyler was recovering so well. Laurel made sure to convey her hopes that their children would soon be healthy again. She hugged Carol before she left, promising to come back and check on Patty, who was still showing gradual signs of improvement.

Only a short while after Tyler was moved to the new room, Jackson left for his job site. He approached the subject very delicately, as if expecting Laurel to be angry with him for leaving, but she waved him off. He really did have to work, she acknowledged, and it wasn't as if there was anything he could do at the hospital.

She tried not to think of her own work being dumped on the other caseworkers because of her absence. Right now it was more important for her to be with Tyler—and as Jackson had pointed out, his job provided Tyler's health insurance.

Now that they were out of ICU, more visitors were allowed. A few of Laurel's friends and co-workers stopped in during the course of the afternoon to ask if she needed anything. Though she assured them all there was nothing she needed, she was genuinely pleased by the sincerity of the offers.

She was even able to greet Beverly Schrader with a warm smile late that afternoon. Tyler, who had been growing tired of the game Laurel was playing with him, welcomed his nanny into the room with a crow of delight.

"Hi, Beb," he said, using the nickname he had given her early in her employment.

"How's my angel?" Beverly approached his bed with a gaily wrapped gift in her hands.

"I had a operation," he told her, pointing toward his chest. "And I got a needle in my arm," he added, glaring at the securely taped IV that he'd been complaining about all day.

"So I see. Your gammy told me you've been very brave. And I heard a nurse say you've been a very good boy."

"Well…pretty good," Tyler muttered with a furtive glance at his mother. He was obviously thinking of a near-tantrum a little while earlier, before they'd begun the game.

"Considering everything, he's been admirably well-behaved." Laurel gave him a smile to show him the earlier lapse was forgiven. After all, there had been a few times during the past couple of days when she'd been perilously close to a tantrum herself.

"I brought you a present, Ty-Ty." Beverly set the box on the bed beside him. "Would you like me to open it for you since you have one hand tied down?"

Though not as vigorous in his enthusiasm for a gift as he normally would have been, Tyler nodded against his pillow. "What is it?"

"Let's see." Sitting on the bed beside him, she efficiently removed the wrapping paper to reveal an equally colorful box. She opened the top and drew out a funny-looking stuffed hamster dressed in scrubs and a stethoscope. It danced and sang a few lines of "Doctor, Doctor" when its tummy was pressed.

Smiling, Tyler immediately reached for the toy, activating the song again. Laurel could tell he was getting sleepy once more, a result of the medications and his lingering post-surgery fatigue. He mumbled a few more comments to Beverly, and then his eyelids seemed to grow too heavy for him to hold open any longer. He fell asleep with the hamster still in his hand and his beloved stuffed penguin tucked into the sheets with him.

"I think he's out." Beverly ran a hand lightly over Tyler's hair as she spoke quietly.

"The pain meds make him sleep a lot still. The doctor said they'll gradually cut back on the dosage during the next few days."

"He seems to be doing remarkably well."

"He really is. He even walked a little this afternoon. They want him to get back into his regular activities as quickly as possible."

"Donna told me you're going to stay home with him from now on."

Rather incongruously, it suddenly occurred to Laurel that Beverly actually looked somewhat like Donna, or maybe the way Donna might have looked more than twenty years ago. Blond, blue-eyed, delicately pretty, obviously intelligent. Why hadn't she noticed the resemblance before?

"I'll be staying with him while he recuperates from the surgery," she agreed somewhat absently. "I'm not sure how long it will be, so I've taken an indefinite leave of absence from work. I know my boss will take me back when I'm ready, since qualified caseworkers are so hard to find."

"Oh. So you *are* planning to go back to work?"

"That's certainly my intention. Not until I'm sure Tyler's fully recovered, of course. I've thought of working only part-time until the fall, when he'll be old enough to enter a good preschool program."

"I see. Donna said—I must have misunderstood her."

Or maybe she hadn't. Laurel wondered just what Donna *had* told Beverly.

Deciding to let that particular subject go, she said, instead, "I'm not sure I've told you how much I appreciate the excellent care you gave Tyler while you worked for us, Beverly. Neither Jackson nor I were aware of the signs you saw that something was wrong with Tyler. I'll always be grateful to you for putting us on alert so that we were able to get early treatment for him. You might very well have saved our son's life."

Beverly looked both pleased and self-conscious in response to Laurel's praise. "I just told you what I suspected. You were the one who took my concerns seriously enough to immediately follow up on them. I'm glad I had some experience with pediatric cardiology while I worked as a nurse's aide."

"So am I," Laurel said fervently. "Will you go back to nursing now, or will you look for another nanny position? I'm more than happy to write a glowing letter of recommendation for you, of course. I'm sure you'll have your choice of employs, since good nannies are even harder to find than social workers."

"Actually, I'd like to go back to school to get my R.N. degree," Beverly admitted. "I mentioned it to your husband the other day, and he seemed to think it was a workable idea. I told him I was worried about having enough money to live on while I'm in school, but he said he's sure there are grants or student loans available for nontraditional nursing students."

Jackson hadn't mentioned the conversation to Laurel. Either he had been so distracted with Tyler that it had slipped his mind, or he'd thought Laurel was too preoccupied to be interested. "I think that's an excellent idea, Beverly. You'd make such an excellent nurse, especially in pediatric care."

"That's what I hope to get into."

"I have some associates through Children's Connection who might know something about student grants or nursing scholarship programs." She was thinking specifically of Leslie Logan, whose charitable activities were almost legendary. Surely Leslie would have some advice to pass on to Beverly. "I'll ask around when I get the chance if you'd like me to."

"I'd really appreciate that. Thank you."

"It's the least I can do. Literally."

Beverly didn't linger much longer. Promising to check on Tyler's progress again, she brushed a kiss across the sleeping child's forehead, then let herself out of the room.

Laurel spent some time after Beverly left berating herself for becoming so irrationally threatened by the nanny during the past few days. She could only chalk up the paranoia to stress and her own vulnerabilities, though neither was a sufficient excuse.

Promising herself she would do everything she could to help Beverly achieve her career goal, she laid her head back against her chair. She should take advantage of Tyler's nap to get some rest, as well. She suspected she was going to need all her energy when he woke again.

Nine

Donna showed up an hour later, rousing Laurel from a light doze. "I'm sorry," she said as she tiptoed into the room. "Did I wake you?"

"No, I wasn't really asleep. Beverly came by earlier and gave Tyler that new toy he's holding."

"That was nice of her. I'm sorry I missed her."

"Did you get all your chores done today?"

Donna turned her face so that Laurel couldn't see her expression. "Yes. How's Tyler?"

"He's been sleeping since Beverly left. He's still making almost miraculous progress, according to everyone here."

"He's a strong little boy. Like his daddy," Donna murmured, laying a hand on Tyler's sheet-covered leg.

"And his grandfather," Laurel added lightly, picturing Carl's solid strength.

Donna raised a hand to her throat. Her fingers trembled visibly as she toyed with the pearl necklace around her neck. Of course Donna wore pearls, Laurel thought wryly. Her hair was always perfect, her makeup was always immaculate, her shoes and purses always matched. It was as if she made a deliberate and concentrated effort to be the perfect "TV mom." Yet now the facade seemed to be developing a few cracks.

Laurel couldn't help wondering why it was so important to Donna to play that impossibly perfect part. And she wondered what was going on behind the flawless mask now.

Maybe she should try to find out what was bothering her mother-in-law. After all, she was a trained social worker, skilled at dealing with other people's problems. But maybe it wasn't her place to pry into Donna's concerns. Maybe Donna would resent her for even trying.

She settled for a tentative, "Is anything wrong, Donna? You seem…troubled."

Donna dropped her hand and straightened her shoulders beneath her tasteful knit top. "Nothing I'm prepared to talk about at the moment."

Well, that was clear enough. Laurel laced her hands in her lap and subsided into silence.

After a moment, Donna sighed. "I didn't mean to sound curt. I suppose I'm just stressed."

Deciding it would be better not to point out that they had all been under stress lately, Laurel merely nodded.

Donna seemed to feel the need to fill the taut silence that lay in the room after their exchange. Sitting on the very edge of the other chair, she cleared her throat a few times, then asked, "Did Beverly tell you she's thinking about returning to nursing school?"

"Yes, she did. I think it's a wonderful idea."

"So do I. Especially since you won't be needing her anymore now that you've quit your job."

"I haven't quit my job. I'm simply taking leave until Tyler's well." She had said the words so often she repeated them almost robotically.

Donna frowned. "You're going back?"

"Donna, I've said all along I planned to return to work. I don't know where you got the idea I wasn't."

"I…well, I just assumed—I mean, you let Beverly go, and Jackson seemed okay with that."

"We let Beverly go because we can't afford to keep paying her while I'm off work for the next couple of months. We didn't think it was fair to keep her dangling without pay, so we told her she should be making other arrangements."

"So Jackson really doesn't mind that you're going back to work?"

"He hasn't said much about it, but I can't imagine why he would mind. This is my decision."

"I would think it's more of a joint decision. As your husband, Jackson should have some say in the matter."

Sometimes the things Donna said nearly made Laurel's jaw drop. This was one of those times.

She shook her head, then spoke candidly, "I really don't get you, Donna. You grew up under modern circumstances, but the world you seem to want to live in hasn't existed in close to fifty years."

Donna toyed with her pearls again. "I know, probably better than you do, exactly what the modern world is like, Laurel. I've seen entirely too much of it. Yet I tried to raise my son in a happy, loving household where he would be sheltered from some of the unpleasantness.

"I married a very traditional man who has supported me, looked after me, loved me more than I perhaps deserved. He loves Jackson with all his heart, and he agreed with me that it was best for Jackson to have a full-time parent in the home. I've been a room mother, PTA president, den mother, field trip chaperone. I've baked cookies and hosted sleepovers and sewn costumes and scrubbed grass stains from sports uniforms. I'm not sure I'd have found time to do all those things if I'd tried to work a full-time job."

Laurel pushed a wisp of hair out of her face as she contemplated Donna's words. She was trying to understand her mother-in-law's viewpoint, just as she wanted Donna to be able to see her side, whether she agreed with it or not.

"I know the difficulties inherent with being a working mother. Every woman's magazine is full of articles about dealing with the guilt and stress and time-management issues. But I know many professional women who have raised happy, successful children. Tyler will always be my first priority, but I feel like my job is important, too. I help other couples find children to love and raise, and not once have I recommended a couple be turned down for an adoption merely because the woman intended to keep working."

Donna shrugged. "You should do what's right for you, of course."

Which could be interpreted to mean that she still didn't approve, but she knew it would serve no purpose to argue. And then she added, "I'll be happy to watch Tyler whenever you need me to. He's always welcome at my house."

"Thank you." Laurel knew she sounded stiff and chilly, but she couldn't seem to help that. "He'll start preschool in August, so that will give him plenty to do while I work."

Donna had heard about the preschool plan before, but that was another touchy subject. "He's so little," she fretted quietly, her gaze still focused on the sleeping child. "It seems so early to— But that decision is yours and Jackson's."

"Yes, it is."

The door opened. In relief, Laurel looked around to see who had interrupted the conversation that had not quite been a quarrel. She had rather hoped it would be Jackson, but Carl walked in, still wearing his rumpled mechanic's uniform. "How's the boy?"

The deep voice roused Tyler from his nap. He squirmed in the bed, then opened his eyes with a momentary frown of confusion that changed to a sleepy smile when he saw his grandparents. "Hi, Gammy. Hi, Gampy."

"Hey, buddy." Carl reached out a callused hand to pat the boy's leg. "How you feeling?"

"Okay." Rubbing his eyes with his free hand, he spoke more alertly. "I got a hamster. It sings. Wanna hear?"

Without waiting for an answer, he squeezed the toy to activate the shrill voice. Carl's expression was comically pained when he looked at Laurel. "Who bought this thing?"

"Beverly. She knew he would be amused by it."

"Or deafened," Carl muttered. He glanced at Donna. "You okay, honey?"

"Yes, I'm fine."

"Did you talk to, um, the person you were planning to talk to today?"

Even Laurel could tell that Donna wasn't pleased by the awkwardly worded question. It seemed particularly to annoy her that he had asked in front of Laurel, since she cast a quick glance her way before replying shortly, "No. I couldn't get through. I'll try again tomorrow."

Subtlety was definitely not one of Carl's strong points. He cleared his throat, looked quickly at Laurel, then clumsily changed the subject. "Jay's not here yet?"

"He's still at work," Laurel said, taking pity on her father-in-law. It was rare that Donna showed annoyance toward her husband, and he obviously regretted that he had displeased her now. "I'm sure he'll be here soon."

"Wonder if that shipment he was waiting on ever came in."

"Yes, I believe it did. I heard him mention it on the phone this morning."

"Good. I know the delay was causing some real problems at the job site."

"So I understand." Suddenly restless and a bit claustrophobic in the room with her in-laws, especially her mother-in-law, Laurel glanced at her watch. "I think I'll leave you two to visit with Tyler for a few minutes while I go have a cup of coffee. I'm having caffeine withdrawal, I'm afraid."

"You go right ahead," Carl urged her, sounding sympathetic. "I know you need to get out of this room sometimes. I'd pretty much go crazy sitting around all day myself."

She knew that. Restless energy was as much a part of Carl as his dry wit and blunt manner of speaking. "Can I get either of you anything while I'm out?"

"Nothing for me, thanks. You need anything, honey?"

Donna shook her head, looking at Carl rather than Laurel. "No. I'm fine."

"I'll be back in a few minutes, Tyler," Laurel said cheerily. And because he had started to frown, she added, "Why don't you play your hamster song for Gampy again?"

"Thanks a lot," Carl grumbled.

Laurel's answering smile lasted only until she was out in the hallway.

Children's Connection was accessible from the hospital by an elevator and a glass-walled walkway. Laurel was actually on her way to the cafeteria when she impulsively switched directions and headed for the foundation instead. She would just pop in for a few minutes to see how things were going, she promised herself.

As late as it was, not many employees would be there, but maybe Morgan had stayed late that day. If he was there, he could bring her up to date on the status of the cases she had been working.

She stepped into the blue-and-white tiled reception area, confirming that the receptionist had already left for the day. The room was decorated for comfort, with plenty of seating, tables arranged with a variety of magazines, and lush plants in large containers. The colors were muted pastels chosen to set visitors immediately at ease.

She shared an office with Maggie Sullivan, another caseworker, who wouldn't be in this late. She decided to check her desk for messages or correspondence that might have accumulated in her absence. She had just moved in that direction when she crossed paths with her least favorite co-worker.

An accountant for the foundation, Everett Baker was in his early to mid-thirties. His dark hair was disarrayed and he had a nervous habit of clearing his throat and shifting his dark eyes away from whoever was speaking to him. Though she had heard he was very good at his work, he tended to be a loner who mingled little with his associates and seemed to make a deliberate effort to blend in with the office furniture. Laurel had tried on occasion to make conversation with him, but she had rarely been successful at drawing more than a few words out of him.

All of her social worker's instincts, combined with her own background, told her that Everett was a man with a lot of heavy baggage. A troubled, maybe even abusive, past. It was something about the way he held himself, as if he were almost anticipating the next blow. But that tiny glimmer of insight—which, for all she knew, could be completely off base—didn't make her any more comfortable around him.

"Leaving for the day?" she asked, settling on meaningless small talk."

He nodded. "I thought you were on leave."

"I just dropped in for a minute to check my messages."

"How's your boy?"

Rather surprised he'd asked, she replied, "He's doing well. Thank you for asking."

"Yeah. Well, see you around."

It was only after he had let himself out that Laurel found herself wondering why he'd been coming out of a hallway that was nowhere near his own office. But because she had so many problems of her own to worry about for now, she quickly pushed odd Everett Baker out of her mind.

Jackson didn't know what had gone on between his wife and his mother while he'd been at work, but the tension between them was unmistakable that evening. More so than usual, anyway.

"Tell me the truth, Dad," he said in frustration as he and his father took a walk around the garden late that evening. "What's going on with Mom? She's been acting…well, weird."

They had left Donna in the waiting room, visiting with some ladies from her Sunday School program who had stopped by the hospital to deliver a fruit basket and ask if there was anything else they could do for the family. Seeing her friends had brought the first natural smile to Donna's face that Jackson had seen in several days.

"Oh, you know, Jay. She's worried about the boy."

Carl was lousy at prevarication. Jackson slanted a frown his way. "C'mon, Dad, I know something's going on. Is Mom sick?"

"No. She's not sick."

Jackson nodded, reassured that his dad was telling the truth that time. "So what is it?"

"If there's anything bothering your mother, it's really up to her to discuss it with you. Not my place to talk behind her back."

"I just want to know if there's anything I can do to help."

"You've got your hands full right now. Your mother will talk to you when—or if—she's ready."

"Just one more question, okay? Is it something *I've* done? Have I hurt her in some way?"

Carl reached out to pat Jackson's shoulder roughly. "You haven't done anything wrong, Jay. Your mother couldn't be prouder of you, and neither could I, for that matter. A man couldn't ask for a better son."

Jackson stopped in his tracks, giving Carl a hard stare. "Are *you* the one who's sick?"

Carl sighed. "I'm not sick. Can't a man pay a compliment to his son without getting attitude?"

"Well, yeah. But you've gotta admit that was a pretty flowery speech coming from you."

"You just remember what I said. And remember I meant every word of it."

"Okay, now you're scaring me. You aren't going to kiss me or anything, are you?"

Carl snorted and punched the shoulder he had patted before. "You always were a smart ass."

Jackson grinned, relieved that Carl sounded more like himself now. He very much needed some things in his life to be normal again.

By Thursday, Laurel wasn't sure whether Jackson was trying too hard to pretend everything was normal in his life, or working like a demon because he was worried about the medical bills that were piling up during Tyler's hospitalization. He had definitely fallen into his old routines, the only difference being that he now came to the hospital after a ten-hour workday rather than going straight home.

To give him credit, he did call a couple of times each day to check on Tyler and ask if Laurel needed anything. And he didn't work as late as he'd been known to in the past, since he was making an effort to be at the hospital before Tyler was down for the night.

Laurel thought of all the days when he had left before Tyler woke in the morning and returned after the boy was asleep. Some of the things Jackson had said during the past few days made her suspect he was thinking the same things too. He made a point to read a book or play a game with Tyler every evening after he arrived at the hospital.

She wondered if that new attitude would survive after Tyler was released. How long would it be until Laurel and Tyler were alone in their house again, waiting for Jackson to take time away from his work to spend with them? When he did come home, he would usually bring stacks of specifications and projections and reports and barricade himself into his home office to pore over them until long after Tyler and Laurel were asleep.

She and Jackson hadn't been alone together since they'd gone home to rest Sunday afternoon. Occasionally she thought she detected the memory of that interlude in his eyes when he looked at her. Maybe he was paying a bit more attention to her opinions? But being on his best behavior while Tyler was in the hospital wasn't necessarily a precursor of major changes in their relationship, she reminded herself. It would be so easy for him—for both of them, she added ruefully—to fall into their old habits of going their own ways, living two separate lives beneath the same roof.

Their relationship hadn't been enough to satisfy her before. She knew full well it hadn't satisfied him, either. More than once during the past year she had wondered if she would be doing him a favor to free him to pursue a woman who was more what he needed. One who didn't bear so many insecurities from childhood. One who would be content to be Mrs. Jackson Reiss and nothing more.

She had told herself when those thoughts had occurred to her in the past that she stayed primarily for Tyler's sake. But deep inside, she knew there was more to it than that. She stayed with Jackson because she had fallen desperately in love with him on that night four years ago, and though many of her perceptions of him had changed since, her love for him had not.

Perhaps she had clung to a fleeting hope that one day he would realize she was exactly what he wanted from a wife even if she didn't—couldn't—be the type of wife he had always envisioned.

No matter his expectation, Laurel couldn't change who she was. Though she didn't resent one minute of the time she spent with Tyler now, there would come a day soon when she would need to go back to work. Already she missed her job—her clients, her co-workers, the emotional rewards she received from helping childless couples.

There was another difference between herself and

Jackson, she mused as she sat in Tyler's room with an unopened book in her lap, waiting for the doctor to make his daily rounds. Laurel worked because she loved her job. Jackson worked for the paycheck.

Although he was interested in the construction industry, he often found it frustrating to be so restricted by the demands and expectations of his overly critical and sometimes unreasonable employer. He had once admitted to Laurel that his dream would be to have his own construction business, a goal that seemed completely out of reach for now.

Though he was careful to save a portion of his earnings, this son of a mechanic and a former waitress lacked the connections and the capital to start up a business. And since social work was hardly a career one entered to get wealthy, he didn't consider Laurel's income sufficient to support the three of them while he took a huge financial risk.

One of Laurel's favorite LPNs, a short, comfortably rounded woman of American Indian descent, entered the room with her usual bright smile, carrying a tray that held a carton of juice and a container of orange sherbet. "I thought you might enjoy a little snack this afternoon, Tyler."

Because Tyler's appetite still hadn't returned, Laurel was pleased when he looked up from his toys with a show of interest. "Ice cream?"

"Close enough," Camilla replied, setting the juice and sherbet on the bed tray. "You can have it as soon as I take your temperature, okay?"

Tyler submitted patiently to having a digital thermometer placed in his ear. Camilla made a note of that reading, which she informed Laurel was normal, then listened to his heart through a stethoscope.

"Everything looks good," she said, looping the stethoscope around the neck of her cartoon-character-decorated scrubs. She rolled the bed tray into position for Tyler and helped him open his sherbet and juice. The despised IV needle was gone now, so Tyler was unimpeded as he dug into the treat eagerly.

Camilla turned to Laurel. "How are you, Mrs. Reiss?"

"Fine, thank you."

"Do you have any questions I can answer? I have a few spare minutes."

"Not just now. I'm still waiting for Dr. Rutledge to come by. He's usually here by now."

"I believe he's running behind today. I heard he had an emergency surgery this morning. Has your regular pediatrician been by yet?"

"This morning. We talked about Tyler's follow-up care. It sounds as though he should be back to normal very quickly."

"You'll be surprised how fast he rebounds. Kids are just amazing in their resiliency."

Laurel laughed a bit ruefully. "He'll probably recover before *I* do. He seems to be taking everything in stride, while I obsess about every little thing."

Camilla made a sympathetic face. "I know. We often tell parents that their children will hardly remember anything of their hospital ordeal, but the parents will recall every tiny detail for the rest of their lives."

"Oh, that's comforting."

"But true," Camilla said pragmatically. And then she

changed the subject. "I haven't seen the rest of your family this afternoon. I hope they're getting some rest."

"My husband had to work today. My mother-in-law had some other things to do." Donna hadn't told Laurel what she would be doing, and Laurel hadn't asked, but she suspected whatever it was had something to do with Donna's recent odd behavior.

"Your in-laws seem nice. Your mother-in-law always makes a point to tell us how satisfied she is with Tyler's care." Camilla wrinkled her short nose. "My own mother-in-law would be criticizing and nitpicking every little thing. That woman is impossible to please, especially when it comes to me."

"You don't get along?" Laurel asked tentatively.

"Oh, well, you know, most married couples face in-law problems at one time or another. It's inevitable, since no two families are exactly alike. It's hard to merge two different backgrounds—different ways of handling money, different religious beliefs and holiday customs, that sort of thing. But out biggest problem is that my mother-in-law never thought I was good enough for her beloved son. She's still telling people our marriage won't last, even thought we just celebrated our twenty-fifth anniversary. And she *never* approved of the way I raised my two kids. But they've turned out to be happy and productive young adults, so I guess I didn't do too bad a job—not that the old bat would ever admit it."

"Did you work while your children were young?" Laurel couldn't resist asking.

"The whole time. My husband and I tried to arrange our schedules so at least one of us was always available for ball games and concerts and teacher conferences, but there were times when work interfered, of course. Our kids had to learn that sometimes we had to take care of our other responsibilities. I think it made them less self-centered, actually. Some kids I see here think the whole world revolves around their pleasure because their folks have spoiled them rotten. And on the other side of the spectrum, others are either abused or neglected by their caretakers. It's just amazing most people survive childhood relatively sane, isn't it?"

Laurel thought of her own basically rudderless upbringing. "I think you're right."

Camilla glanced at Tyler. "Your little boy sure hasn't caused us any trouble. He's so well-behaved. He's lucky to have a loving family around him."

Laurel told herself she would remember those words whenever she became too frustrated with Donna. There was no question that it was good for Tyler to have his extended family nearby. Tyler's needs came first, she vowed. If there were some needs of her own that weren't being entirely fulfilled… Well, she was used to that. She had learned long ago to be content with what she had.

After all, she thought, happily-ever-after endings only happened in fairy tales.

Ten

Tyler was taken for a physical therapy session Thursday afternoon, which basically consisted of supervised play with other pediatric surgery patients. Having been informed that he would be gone for about half an hour, Laurel decided to pop over to Children's Connection, just to check in.

She was halfway down the connecting hallway when she came face to face with Leslie Logan. As elegantly coordinated as always, Leslie stopped in her tracks when she spotted Laurel. "Laurel! How's little Tyler today?"

Laurel smiled broadly as she relayed the news she had received only an hour earlier. "We're taking him home tomorrow."

"Oh, my goodness, that's wonderful! I'm sure you're

counting the minutes. I've heard you've barely left the hospital during the past week."

"As nice as everyone has been to us, I'm more than ready to be home," Laurel admitted. "Do you know how hard it is to actually get any sleep in a hospital?"

"I've had a few personal experiences. Enough to know I'm in no hurry to be hospitalized again anytime soon."

Leslie changed the subject then. "Laurel, I was hoping to speak to you soon, at your convenience, of course. I have a little favor to ask of you."

"A favor?" Though surprised that Leslie Logan would need anything from her, she couldn't imagine turning her down. Leslie had always been so supportive of Children's Connection, and of Laurel, personally. "Anything. Just name it."

Obviously touched by Laurel's immediate reply, Leslie reached out to lay a perfectly manicured hand on Laurel's arm. "Actually, I need your services as a social worker. I know you've taken a leave of absence, but maybe you could do the preliminary paperwork for one case? The interviews could even take place in your home, if necessary. I know what I'm asking is hardly standard operating procedure, but this is a special case."

"I don't understand."

Leslie looked around, seemingly to make sure no one was listening. "My daughter, Bridget, and her new husband, Sam, are interested in adopting a baby. I'm not asking you to give them any special preference or to cut any legal corners. They'll go through procedures, then wait their turn like anyone else. But if you can find the time, I would appreciate if you conduct the early interviews."

"Why me?" Laurel asked curiously.

"Bridget's a little nervous about the whole process," Leslie confided with an indulgent laugh that had an oddly false ring to it. "I told her I believe you're just the person to put both her and Sam at ease about all the red tape and paperwork."

"Well, I…"

"As I said, I know this is completely unorthodox for me to approach you this way, especially at such a stressful time. Please feel free to say no if you don't think you can do this. I promise I won't hold it against you," Leslie promised with a smile that looked strained.

"Give me a call next week and we'll discuss a time for a preliminary interview," Laurel said after only a momentary hesitation. "I'm sure we'll be able to work something out."

Leslie squeezed Laurel's arm in a quick gesture of appreciation before stepping away. "Thank you, Laurel. And please let me know if there's anything I can do for you during your son's recuperation."

Okay, Laurel thought. Now *that* was weird. If she hadn't been so crazy about Leslie, she'd have turned that odd proposition down flat. After all, she was on leave. And Leslie had been right about the request being totally unorthodox.

Shaking her head in bemusement, she moved on toward her office.

Jackson entered Tyler's hospital room late Thursday evening with a combination of guilt and dread. It was almost nine o'clock, and he knew Laurel would be annoyed with him for coming so late. At least she wouldn't yell at him in front of Tyler; she'd probably "invite" him out of the room to do that.

Already in defensive mode, he met her eyes the moment he entered the room, though he greeted Tyler first. "Hey, sport. How'd everything go today?"

"I'm going home," Tyler announced happily, bouncing on the end of the bed where he'd sat watching television, his penguin and new hamster sitting on either side of him.

"Are you?" Jackson looked from him back to Laurel again. "When?"

"Tomorrow," Laurel said. "Both the surgeon and the pediatrician told me there was no need to keep him here any longer."

As he had expected, her voice had just a hint of a chill to it, but there was something else, too. Something that made him suspect she was more disappointed in him than angry. That made him feel even worse than he had before, which, of course, only made him more defensive.

Jackson swung his son off the bed and into his arms, taking a bit more care than usual as he hugged him. "It will be so good to have you home again."

Laurel made a sound deep in her throat, then seemed to swallow whatever she had almost blurted out. Probably something about how Tyler would be home but Jackson probably wouldn't be.

"I tried to call you after the doctor left," she said after a moment, "but your cell phone was off."

"I forgot to recharge the battery last night. When I checked it this afternoon it was completely dead. I meant to call you from another phone, but everything was so chaotic today I never had the chance."

"I'm sure you thought you were needed where you were."

Her prim tone made his jaw set. "Yes, I was needed. I had two men injured this afternoon when a scaffolding collapsed. After they were taken by ambulance from the site, we had to inspect all the rest of the scaffolding and then reconstruct the section that fell."

Her expression eased just a bit. "How badly were they injured?"

"They'll be okay." He was the one who sounded stiff now. "Bob Cooper broke his leg, and Howie Young probably has a concussion and some broken ribs."

"I'm sorry. Do you know what caused the collapse?"

"Yeah. Stupid mistakes."

"Made while you were here at the hospital, I suppose, and not there to micromanage every detail."

"You got it." He set Tyler back on the bed. "And who do you think will take the blame for it?"

"Your boss won't blame you for taking care of your son."

"Hmm." Because he knew his boss better than she did, he didn't bother to argue. But then he conceded, "I should have called you."

Relenting a little, she shrugged. "I can understand why you didn't. It must have been a terrible afternoon for you."

"Hearing that Tyler's going home makes up for it. Damn, it'll be good to have him home again."

Tyler looked up from the TV to frown repressively at his father. "You don't supposed to say that word, Daddy."

Jackson grinned and ruffled Tyler's hair. "You're

right, sport. I'm not. Do you think your mommy's going to make me stand in the time-out corner?"

Laurel laughed—probably for Tyler's sake, Jackson thought. "I'll just give you a warning this time."

He moved to sit in the other visitor's chair. He glanced at the cartoon that seemed to be holding Tyler's attention as he asked Laurel, "Have my parents already left for the evening?"

"Yes. Your mother said she had a headache. Carl talked her into going home a little early tonight."

Despite the reassurance he'd felt about his mother's health after his talk with Carl, Jackson began to worry again that she was ill. She'd never been one to suffer from headaches. "I don't suppose she's talked to you any more about what's been bothering her?"

"To me? Hardly."

"Have you tried asking her?"

"Yes, I've tried. She wouldn't say a word."

He could only hope his mother would be back to normal tomorrow, after Tyler was home and safe. Despite the complaints he'd had about his job and his marriage, it seemed that now all he really wanted was for things to go back to the way they were before.

Maybe a few small things had changed, he thought—or, more accurately, hoped. Maybe he and Laurel had settled a few issues. Maybe they'd been brought a little closer together during this crisis with their son.

Glancing at her out of the corner of his eye, he saw that her face was almost expressionless, her gaze focused on Tyler, her lower lip protruding just slightly, the way it did when she was deep in thought about something. And he realized he didn't have a clue what she was thinking. Once again, she could have almost been a stranger sitting in the room with him. So maybe they hadn't solved their problems, after all.

What was with the women in his life, anyway? How come they were both so distant from him lately? He was almost used to it from Laurel, but his mother had always been forthcoming with him. He'd never had the feeling that she was hiding things from him—until this past week, anyway.

Was it something he was doing that was driving them away? If so, he sure as hell wished they would tell him what it was, he thought wearily, the stress of a hard day making itself felt in the knotted muscles at the back of his neck. He could use a massage himself.

Glancing at his wife again, he thought ruefully that there was no hope for help from that direction tonight.

He stayed a couple of hours, until Tyler was ready to go to sleep for the night. Laurel assured him there was no need for him to remain any longer. "We'll be fine here for one more night."

"You're sure you don't need me to stay?" He had offered several times to be the one to spend the night in Tyler's room and allow Laurel to go home and sleep in her own bed, but she refused even to consider it.

She nodded to Tyler as the boy gave a huge, noisy yawn. "He won't be awake much longer. The nurses will be in soon to get him settled for the night and to bring clean sheets for me."

"What time will he be released tomorrow?"

"The doctor said sometime after ten. Camilla told me to expect a lengthy check-out process, since so many patients are released on Friday. It could be several hours of waiting."

"I'll be here to take you home. I'll run by the site early and be here by ten."

"You're sure you can get away?"

"To take my son home from the hospital?" It rather annoyed him that she had even asked. "I'll be here."

"All right. I'll call if anything changes."

"Right. I'll remember to charge the cell phone tonight. Do you need me to bring you anything tomorrow?"

"I'm good. I still have the extra clean clothes you brought yesterday."

"Okay. Then I'll see you both tomorrow." He leaned over to kiss his wife, noting that frustrating hesitation in her response again. And then he kissed Tyler, pleased that at least his son held nothing back in his goodnight embrace.

As he stepped into his dark, empty house a while later, he thought with relief how nice it would be to come home to his family again. Even if they were already asleep, he thought with a self-directed grimace and a vow that he would try not to spend so many nights working when he should be taking time with his son. The son he could so easily have lost, he reminded himself.

And as he climbed into his empty bed, he wondered how many more nights he would have to sleep in it alone. Would things really be different when Laurel and Tyler came home? His son was being returned to him—but had he already lost his wife?

Laurel was almost giddy with anticipation Friday morning. She was taking her son home. Every medical professional she had spoken to had assured her that he was recovering phenomenally well from his surgery and had every reason to expect a long, healthy life. Though his activities would be slightly limited for the next two weeks, until his post-surgery checkup, he would be free after that to be as active as any other boy.

She worried a little about being responsible for his care now, of course. She had come to depend on the nurses and staff who had hovered so protectively over him during the past week. But they had all promised her she had nothing to be troubled about.

She had memorized the list of instructions but still worried whether she was up to the responsibility. It was that same old demon that had haunted her from the beginning—the one that taunted her with the possibility that she was no more fit to be a mother than her own had been.

It irritated her that she still fought those groundless fears. A strong, competent woman should be able to rid herself of the baggage from her past, shouldn't she? Feeling scared and inadequate so much of the time seemed to her to be a sign of weakness. And she didn't try to place any of the blame for her insecurities on Jackson or Donna. She knew she wouldn't allow herself to be shaken by their expectations if she had enough confidence in her own capabilities.

"You'll be fine, Mrs. Reiss," Camilla assured her. "You both will," she added with a smile for Tyler. "But if you have any questions at all, feel free to call any of the nursing staff here, okay?"

"I'll do that. Thank you so much."

Camilla reached out to give Laurel a quick hug.

"Sometimes the parents up here need a little TLC themselves," she said understandingly.

Laurel returned the hug warmly. "I can't thank you enough for everything you've done for us these past few days. I'll be sure and let the administration know what wonderful nurses they have working this wing."

"You do that." Camilla drew away and turned toward the door. "Well, good morning, Mr. Reiss. Ready to take your boy home?"

Laurel felt her smile fade a bit as she met Jackson's eyes. He kept his own firmly in place when he spoke to the nurse. "You bet I am. Is he ready to go yet?"

"Oh, we still have to finish the paperwork and get the doctor's signature. You should know our motto by now—everything happens at the doctor's convenience, not the rest of us. But you can be taking his things out to your car if you'd like. That might save you a little trouble later."

Jackson and Laurel spent the next few minutes packing up Tyler's clothes and toiletries, along with the toys, books and games people had brought to entertain him. He refused to let go of his penguin or his hamster, but he allowed everything else to be packed with the promise that he could play with them again when he was home.

In addition to his belongings, there were several balloon and flower arrangements sent by friends and co-workers, and the remains of another fruit basket provided by Donna's neighbors. Jackson had to borrow a wheeled cart from the nurses just to get everything moved to his car, which he'd parked in the deck.

By the time Jackson returned, Tyler was almost

ready to go. Dressed in a thin red hoodie with jeans and sneakers, he looked so much back to normal that it brought a hard lump to Laurel's throat.

She watched as the entire staff from the wing told him goodbye in a cheery ceremony that probably took place several times a day. She knew it must bring joy to the nurses to watch their little charges going home so happy and healthy, when all too often there was a different outcome. She wondered how they were able to deal with losing any of their precious patients. In their place she was afraid she would get too attached. She'd always believed it took a special person to be a nurse, but after the past week, she was sure of it.

Tyler thoroughly enjoyed the wheelchair ride to the car. Buckled securely into his car seat, he talked incessantly all the way home, which saved Laurel and Jackson the need to make conversation.

Leaving the baggage to be retrieved later, Jackson carried Tyler into their house on his back, making an elaborate production out of the pony ride. Tyler squealed in delight, holding on to his father's broad shoulders, happy to be home.

Carrying an armload of flowers, Laurel hovered close behind, trying not to be overprotective, but mindful of the need to protect Tyler's incision. She knew Jackson was being careful, but she couldn't forget the doctor's warning that Tyler shouldn't engage in any activities where he could hit his chest. No climbing trees, hanging from jungle gyms, riding his bike, contact sports or wrestling with other children for the next two months, she mentally recited. No limits on stair climbing or regular play, but he should be encouraged to nap if he was tired.

And there were no limits on pony rides from his daddy, she added, forcing herself to relax. Laughter had to be as good for him as any medicine.

"I'm home, I'm home, I'm home," Tyler chanted, bouncing on Jackson's shoulders.

Swinging the boy to the floor, Jackson grinned broadly. "I take it you're glad to be back."

Tyler nodded happily. "Can we go to the zoo now?"

Laurel couldn't help laughing at the way Jackson's jaw dropped. "So much for savoring his homecoming."

"We'll go to the zoo another time, okay, sport? Right now you'd better go see your fish. They've been missing you like crazy."

"Okay." Tyler dashed toward his room, dragging his penguin behind him.

Pushing a hand through his hair, which Tyler had left standing in spikes, Jackson turned back toward the door. "I'll get the rest of the stuff."

"I'll go check on Tyler and then start lunch. I'm sure I already know what he wants."

"Macaroni and cheese?"

"Bingo." Anyone who knew Tyler was aware that he loved boxed macaroni and cheese almost as much as ice cream.

Jackson cleared his throat. "As appetizing as that sounds, I won't be able to stay for lunch, I'm afraid. I have to get back to work. You'll, um, be okay here?"

"Of course I'll be okay. I'm home."

She didn't resent that he was going to work today, she assured herself. After everything that had happened on his job yesterday, she knew he'd done well to take even a few hours today. And hadn't she promised Leslie Logan that she would work a case next week, even though she was officially on a leave of absence?

"I'm sure Mom will be over in a little while to help out."

"She's welcome to visit, of course, but I really don't need any help. I'm just going to throw some laundry in while Tyler plays. I'm sure he'll need some extra attention, but I don't have anything else pressing to do other than play with him or read to him."

"I'll be home in time to read him a bedtime story," Jackson promised. "I'll try to be no later than seven."

She nodded. "I'll have dinner ready. As good as the hospital food is, it will be nice to eat something that doesn't come from the cafeteria for a change."

"I'll second that." He leaned over to give her a light goodbye kiss, then paused for another, slightly longer one. "It's good to have you home. I've missed you."

She swallowed. "I've missed you, too," she murmured.

She doubted he knew she was talking about missing him for much longer than the last few days. But maybe things would be better now, she thought with a flicker of wary optimism.

Just maybe...

Jackson hadn't been gone for an hour before Donna showed up at the front door. Laurel let her in with the usual reserved courtesy. "Tyler's lying down for a little while. He got overexcited about coming home and used up his strength. I don't expect him to sleep long, though. Can I get you some coffee while we wait for him to wake up?"

"Do you have any decaf?"

"Just made a fresh pot. I was going to have a cup with a slice of chocolate cake my neighbor brought over a few minutes ago."

"That was nice of her. Was it Mrs. Pelotti?"

"Yes."

Donna nodded. "Beverly was always fond of her. They shared coffee together often during Tyler's nap-time."

It took some effort, but Laurel kept her smile firmly in place. "Yes, so I've heard."

Donna declined any cake, and she barely touched her coffee while Laurel ate her own cake and tried to think of things to say. Laurel had the feeling there was something her mother-in-law wanted to bring up but was hesitant to do so. She decided to keep talking about inconsequential matters and let Donna take her own time in directing the conversation elsewhere.

When Donna did finally speak, her question caught Laurel off-guard. "Am I right in thinking that you and Jackson have been getting along better lately?"

Laurel lifted her eyebrows. "I beg your pardon?"

"You think I'm prying into your marriage." Donna seemed to have been prepared for that possibility. "It just seems to me that the two of you have grown a bit closer during Tyler's ordeal."

"It's been my observation that parents either grow closer or completely fall apart during a child's illness," Laurel said with a slight shrug. "Jackson and I chose to cope with the stress together. As a team," she added, quoting him.

"You seemed to let him take care of you more while

you were pretty much trapped at the hospital during the past week. He needs to feel that he's taking care of his family, you know. Most men see themselves as protectors and providers, and when that role is taken away from them, they become insecure."

"Haven't we already had this conversation? If you're going to try to pressure me again into quitting my job so Jackson can be secure in his 'manly' role, then—"

"I'm not trying to pressure you into anything," Donna interrupted impatiently. "I just wanted to tell you that I hope you and he are working out your problems. A wife is her husband's safe refuge when he runs into hard times. She makes herself available when he needs to feel loved and reassured. And before you ask, no, he doesn't talk to me about any problems between the two of you. I just know him so well that I can sense when he isn't entirely happy."

She made it clear enough that she thought she knew her son of thirty-plus years better than his wife of four years did. And probably that was true, in some ways, Laurel thought. But Donna didn't know *her* very well at all. Laurel wanted to believe that was as much Donna's fault as it was her own.

They weren't the only mother- and daughter-in-law who felt the need to compete for their son and husband's love and attention, she was certain. She'd read enough magazine articles dealing with that subject. But none of those articles had seemed to quite address Donna's hot and cold attitude, or Laurel's feeling that Donna always seemed to know something that no one else did.

Maybe Laurel and Jackson had grown a bit closer during Tyler's illness, but the same couldn't be said about Laurel and Donna. In fact, Laurel felt more tense around her mother-in-law now than she ever had before. Knowing how close Jackson was to his parents, she didn't think it boded well for the marriage that her relationship with his mother was falling apart. How could they truly be a team if they were so often on opposing sides?

As she had predicted, Tyler's nap didn't last long. He came into the kitchen with the color returned to his face and a renewed spring to his step, his eyes lighting up when he saw the chocolate cake and his grandmother, in that order.

There was no further opportunity for Laurel and Donna to talk privately, and Laurel was glad. They never seemed to accomplish much with their candid discussions.

It was only much later that she thought of Donna's words and wondered if there had been a warning for her in them. Was Donna expecting Jackson to face something that would leave him needing the support of a loving wife? Something that had nothing to do with Tyler's illness?

Was Donna finally going to talk to Jackson about whatever she had been hiding from him?

Eleven

Having been summoned by his mother, Jackson stopped by his parents' house after leaving the job site Saturday afternoon. He called Laurel to let her know where he would be, and something in her voice when she replied warned him to brace himself. Either she knew something or, like Jackson, she was guessing that Donna was ready to talk—and that it wasn't going to be a casual conversation.

"Tyler and I are fine," she'd told him as they concluded the call. "You spend all the time you need with your parents. I— Well, I think something's wrong with your mother."

Because her words so closely echoed his own concerns, he pulled into his parents' driveway with a tight knot of dread in his stomach. Maybe it was nothing, he tried to convince himself. Maybe they just wanted to see him.

Knowing his dad, they were probably going to offer money for medical bills or something. That sort of thing would embarrass all of them, and Jackson wouldn't even consider accepting, but it would be typical of Carl to make the attempt.

That had to be what it was about, he decided as he loped up their front steps. Money had always been an awkward subject between them. Donna said it was because both her men had so much stiff-necked pride.

But when Donna let him in, it turned out Carl wasn't even home. "He's at his shop," Donna explained, her face pale, her movements unmistakably jittery. "We both thought it would be better if I talked to you alone."

The knot in his stomach twisted tighter. He was surprised that his voice sounded so calm when he asked, "What's going on, Mom?"

"Come into the den and let's sit down. It will be easier to talk if we're comfortable."

Though Jackson didn't think he was going to get comfortable in any way until he knew what this was all about, he followed her into the wood-paneled family room. A sense of familiarity immediately flooded through him. This was home. The place where he'd grown up. Where he'd crashed on the floor to watch TV or piled on the sofas with his friends or wrestled on the rug with his dogs.

The décor hadn't changed much since he'd moved out. The same slightly dented oak tables. The same prints of landscapes and wildlife. The same framed photographs of him in boyhood uniforms and cap and gown. The lopsided ceramic vase he'd made his mother in a required junior-high art class, and which she still kept in a place of honor on the oak mantel. The uphol-stered furniture had been replaced through the years, but even the new pieces were covered in the same earthy colors as before.

Home.

Donna settled on one end of the big, deeply cush-ioned brown couch, and he sat beside her, half turned to face her. His eyes focused on her drawn face, he said, "All right, Mom, out with it. What's wrong? Are you ill?"

"No." She reached out to cover his clenched fist with her hand, which felt icy against his skin. "I'm not sick. I've just— Well, I have something to tell you, darling. And it's hard. The hardest thing I've ever had to face."

His throat clenched. "Dad? Is he—"

"He's fine," she said quickly. "This has nothing to do with our health."

"Then what is it?" It was all he could do not to snap. The tension was getting to be too much for him.

She drew a deep breath that ended in what might have been a choked sob. "You're going to hate me."

"Mom." He caught her hands between both of his, squeezing them firmly enough to make her wince a lit-tle. Easing up, he said, "Nothing you could say—noth-ing—would make me hate you. Got that?"

She nodded, but she didn't look convinced.

A dozen potential explanations had been swirling through his mind, some of them crazy, some more pos-sible. One of them suddenly seemed to make sense in context with what she'd just said. "Are you leaving Dad?"

"Leave Carl?" It was obvious that she was shocked at the very suggestion. "Of course not. I could never leave Carl. I love him. And I owe him everything—my very life, for that matter. If it hadn't been for him—" She choked again.

Okay, so that was one scenario he could quit worrying about.

"Look, I could sit here all day trying to guess what you need to tell me, but it would save us both a lot of time and trouble if you'd just blurt it out."

Donna drew a deep breath that must have burned a path all the way down to her lungs, judging from her pained expression. "I guess I've told you that I had kind of a hard-knock life growing up. I was a vain, rebellious teenager who didn't get along well with my mother or stepfather or my two younger half-brothers. I ran with the wrong crowd, did plenty of things I shouldn't have, got in trouble at school and even with the law at times. I came very close to going to jail on a couple of occasions."

She'd told him she had been an undisciplined teen, more as a warning to him than for any other reason, but he hadn't realized quite how far she had gone in her rebellion. This was the first he'd heard of any real trouble.

"I've got to admit it's hard for me to imagine you being a wild teenager, but that certainly doesn't change the way I feel about you now, except to make me admire you even more for turning your life around the way you did."

Donna looked down at their joined hands. "The credit for that goes to Carl. He rescued me from a situation that seemed so hopeless that I was considering suicide."

That shocked him. "Good God, Mom, what happened to you?"

"I was stupid. And naive. And so very blind." She drew another shuddering breath. "It started when I was barely nineteen. I'd gotten a job working in a rather seedy diner downtown. I blew every penny I earned on clothes and partying—and I made good tips because I was a pretty young blond who didn't mind flirting with leering old men."

Jackson didn't want to know if she'd gone beyond flirting with those old men for extra tips. Instead, he said, "You told me you met Dad when you were working as a waitress and he was a customer."

She nodded. "Your dad was a regular in the diner before I even started there. He worked in someone else's mechanic shop then, and all I saw when I looked at him was a shy, blue-collar worker almost ten years older than me. He wasn't movie-screen handsome, and he didn't make much more than I did, so I have to confess I wasn't romantically interested in him, even though I knew he had a crush on me almost from the start."

She choked a little. "So blind," she whispered, sounding far away—more than thirty years in the past, Jackson figured.

He stayed quiet, knowing she would continue when she was ready, but keeping a supporting hold on her cold, trembling hands.

"One morning this man came in for coffee. Oh, he was something. Blond, blue-eyed, tanned. Expensive clothes and a way of carrying himself that let everyone know he was somebody important. He was in his mid-thirties—seventeen years older than I was. I took one look at him and I fell hard. I'm pretty sure I made a fool of myself fawning all over him, flirting and flaunting myself at him. When he left, he tipped me twenty dollars for a three-dollar order of pie and coffee. I spent the rest of the morning giggling and daydreaming about him. The next day he came back."

It wasn't hard to guess where the story was leading. His jaw clenched, Jackson nodded for her to go on.

"He was married," she said flatly. "He had children. But he told me his marriage was an unhappy one, and that his wife was a cold, bitter woman who didn't understand him. I fell for it like the silly, shallow teenager I was.

"I was his mistress for almost two years. I suspected that I wasn't the only one, but I refused to believe it, because the things he said to me sounded so perfect and sincere. He told me he would leave his wife as soon as he could do so without causing too much pain to his kids."

She swallowed audibly. "He gave me money, but he wanted me to keep my job at the diner. I didn't ask him why, but I kept working. I saw Carl there almost every day. He knew I was headed for big trouble, and he tried to warn me, but I wouldn't listen. I liked him a great deal, considered him a friend, but I was too stupid then to know the difference between a real, decent man and a flashy, selfish opportunist."

"You're being awfully hard on yourself, Mom," Jackson murmured. "You were just a kid, for crying out loud."

"I should have known better," she argued flatly. "I *did* know better. But I didn't care about his wife or his kids. I wanted him to marry me. I wanted the money, the prestige, the good life he shared with them. The more demanding I became, the further he drew away. Until he quit coming around all together. I hounded him, chased after him, begged him. We had a big scene when he told me it was over. I was devastated."

"And that's when you turned to Dad?"

"Oh, sweetheart." She swallowed, then said woodenly, "A few weeks after the big break-up, I realized I was pregnant."

Jackson's heart fell into the pit of his stomach. Acting on blind instinct, he released her hands and sprang to his feet, shoving his fists into the pockets of his jeans.

A startled curse escaped him in a hiss. His mother didn't even bother to reprimand him for it, as she would have at any other time.

Several long moments passed while Jackson tried to deal with all the implications of her admission. And then Donna spoke again, her voice barely recognizable. "I waited until it was too late for an abortion before I contacted him again. I was convinced he would leave his wife and family then. It never occurred to me that he would refuse even to talk to me. I got a note from him denying that he was the father of my child, threatening to expose me as a slut and a gold digger, and ordering me to stay away from him. I received that letter on my twenty-first birthday. I was almost six months pregnant."

The sound that escaped Jackson then sounded much like a growl. He couldn't seem to make himself look at her now. He stood with his back half turned to her, his head down.

Donna didn't give him time to speak before she forged on. There was no emotion at all in her voice now, just an obvious determination to finish this. "Carl was worried about me. He came to my apartment to check on me, and he found me unconscious. I had taken a handful of pills. The letter I had received was lying beside me.

"He rushed me to the hospital, where the staff saved my life…and yours. Carl has always said you must have had a really efficient guardian angel, because you survived that to develop into a full-term seven-and-a-half pound baby, and because you were never seriously injured in any of the reckless stunts you pulled as an active, growing boy."

Carl, Jackson thought with a hard swallow. The dad he had grown up idolizing and emulating. The man he now knew was not his biological father.

Donna moistened her lips before saying, "Carl convinced me to marry him a few days after I was released from the hospital. I was scared and depressed and lost, and he wanted to take care of me. He hasn't stopped taking care of me—of us—since. He loved me without question. He loved you with all his heart from the moment he first held you in his arms. And before our first anniversary had passed, I had learned the difference between obsessive infatuation and true love."

A stranger's voice came from Jackson's mouth when he asked, "Why are you telling me this now?"

And why the hell haven't you told me before?

"I figured it was inevitable that you would start asking more questions about blood types and genetic history. That there was a risk you would figure it out for yourself. And I thought both you and Tyler deserved to know what other medical conditions you might have inherited.

"I contacted the man who fathered you and asked him about the heart defect. He admitted that he's had heart problems himself, and that he lost several cousins and uncles to early heart attacks—a couple who were only in their early twenties. He's going to warn his other children to watch for the condition in their families and to be screened for the defect themselves."

His other children. Jackson's half-siblings. He couldn't go there right now. "I need to think about this."

"I know. But I need to tell you one more thing. You should know who your real father is."

For the first time since he'd been a kid, Jackson wanted to yell at his mother. He wanted to shout at her that his real father was Carl Reiss. And he wanted more than he had ever wanted anything in his life for it to be the truth. "I don't care what his name is."

"You need to know," she insisted. "It's Jack Crosby."

It took him a moment to place the name. And then he scowled. "The computer millionaire?"

"Yes. He has become a very wealthy, powerful man. He's almost seventy now, married to his second wife, who's much younger than he is, of course. And he wants to meet you."

"Jack Crosby." Repeating the name made him almost sick to his stomach. "You named me after him, damn it!"

She nodded miserably. "At the time it seemed like a

way of defying him. Of disputing that horrible letter and proclaiming that you were his son, despite anything he claimed. Carl suggested I might want to give you another name, to spare me the pain and you the embarrassment when the truth came out, but I wouldn't listen. I was still so angry."

"You must have hated him. And me."

"I didn't hate you," she protested instantly. And then she gave a little cry and added, "Or maybe I did. I was such an emotional mess then that I didn't know what I felt. Carl helped me get past that anger and I fell in love with you even as I grew to love him. I adore you, Jackson. And so does your dad. Surely you can't doubt that now."

No wonder Carl had always called him Jay. Or son or buddy or pal—anything but his real name. He pressed a hand to his stomach, suddenly afraid he was going to vomit right on his mother's spotless carpet.

"I've got to go," he said, turning on one heel toward the door. "I need to…"

What? What could he do to make this any better? "I need to think," he finished, moving in long, urgent strides. "I'll talk to you later."

His mother didn't try to stop him. As he let himself out the front door, he thought he heard soft sobs coming from behind him. He didn't pause long enough to find out for certain.

It was almost ten o'clock Saturday evening when Laurel called her in-laws' number. She was relieved when Carl, rather than Donna, answered.

"Carl, it's Laurel. Is Jackson there?"

"No, he's not here. I— We were hoping he'd gone home."

"I haven't heard from him since he called early this afternoon and told me he was stopping by your house. I've tried calling his cell phone, but apparently he's got it turned off."

"He left here quite awhile ago. Maybe he went to the job site or something."

He sounded as doubtful as she was about that possibility. Something told her there was more to Jackson's absence than work. After all, he had told her that he was finished at the site for the day and would be coming home after his visit with his parents. He had planned to spend some time with Tyler before bedtime.

Tyler had been asleep for more than an hour now. Surely Jackson would have called if he had simply changed his mind.

"Carl, did something happen there to upset him?" she asked, trying to phrase her words carefully. "When he left, did he seem okay?"

"I, er, wasn't here when Jay left. He'd been talking with his mother."

Laurel's hand tightened around the telephone receiver. "Did she say anything about where he was going when he left?"

"No. But, Laurel, he *was* upset."

"How upset?"

"Very."

She moistened her lips. "Can you tell me why?"

"I'd better leave that to Jay or Donna. I'm sure he just needs some time alone to think about some things, you know?"

"I'm worried about him, Carl. It's not like him just to disappear this way. Not when he isn't working, anyway."

"He'll show up." Carl was obviously trying to reassure himself as well as her. "Just give him some time."

As she hung up the phone, Laurel wondered just how much time she was supposed to give him. All night? All weekend?

She thought about calling a couple of his friends, but she suspected the calls would be fruitless. She doubted that Jackson had left his mother's house in turmoil only to go shoot pool or play a game of pick-up basketball with his pals.

She paced. Just what had Donna told him? Had Laurel been right about her initial guess that he'd been adopted? She knew that wasn't easy news for an adult to hear. Family secrets were almost impossible to keep forever, and in her experience, the sooner they were out in the open the better.

It that was it, maybe she could help him deal with it. It was what she did for a living, right? She could assure him that the adoptive parents she worked with loved their children every bit as much as those who had conceived biologically.

Of course, she wouldn't be able to help him if he didn't first admit that he needed help. There was little she could do if he went all quiet and macho on her—which he seemed to be doing even now—hiding his feelings, insisting he could deal with everything on his own, sublimating his own insecurities by being even more determined to be the strong man in charge of his household.

She hated to think that this latest crisis could drive the final wedge between them, but she knew it very well could unless they both made every effort really to communicate this time.

She would do her best, she vowed. Whatever the problem turned out to be. But she couldn't do anything if he didn't come home.

Another half hour passed. She thought about calling Donna, demanding to know what had gone on between her and Jackson. She thought about calling local hospitals to make sure he wasn't hurt, or worse. She thought about calling the police. She actually had her hand on the phone, though she didn't have a clue whose number she planned to dial, when she heard the back door open.

Exhaling in relief, she moved away from the phone, hurrying toward the kitchen, which connected to the garage. "Jackson?"

She found him standing in the darkened kitchen, his expression that of a man who had wandered into the wrong house by mistake. "Jackson?" she repeated, turning on the light and making him blink. "Are you all right? Where have you been?"

"I, uh, I've been out. Driving," he added, sounding as confused as he looked.

She frowned. "Have you been drinking?"

She'd never known him to drown his problems in alcohol, a crutch Carl had taught him to avoid. She certainly didn't want to think of him driving under the influence, endangering himself and everyone else on the roadways. But he didn't sound like himself.

He moved then, tossing his keys on the table and

shoving a hand through his hair. "No, I haven't been drinking. Just driving."

"Have you had anything to eat?"

He seemed to make an effort to remember before replying, "No."

"I made dinner. I'll put a plate in the microwave for you."

"I'm not hungry."

She opened the refrigerator door. "You need to eat."

"Maybe something to drink."

"There's iced tea," she said, setting a covered plate of pot roast and vegetables in the microwave. Maybe the aromas would make him hungry, she thought as she poured tea into a glass. "Sit down. Your dinner will be ready in two minutes."

Automatically following instructions, he sat, lacing his fingers on the table in front of him. He didn't move when she set his tea beside his hands. She hesitated a moment, then turned to get out silverware and a napkin.

As often as she had wished Jackson would let her see him in his vulnerability, she found herself shaken by the lost look in his eyes. Maybe she had come to depend on a strong Jackson more than she had realized.

He still hadn't moved when she brought his reheated dinner to him. "Move your hands, Jackson," she said quietly.

He pulled them off the table, allowing her to set the plate in front of him.

"Now eat."

He looked at the plate as if he couldn't remember exactly how to begin.

Her heart in her throat, she picked up his fork and put it in his hand. "Eat."

She watched as he complied again. She suspected that he might as well be swallowing chalk for all the enthusiasm he showed. Sitting across the table, she waited until he'd eaten enough to satisfy her before asking, "Are you okay?"

"I'm fine."

The clipped tone didn't encourage any further questions. She tried again, anyway. "Maybe we should call your parents and let them know you're okay. Your dad sounded a little worried when I talked to him earlier."

He didn't look up from his plate. "Did he?"

"Yes. He, um, said he thought you were upset after your talk with your mother."

"He was right."

"Are you going to tell me about it?"

"I'll have to, eventually. But I don't want to talk about it now."

"Is your mother all right?"

"Oh, yeah. She's just fine."

Anger, she thought, analyzing his tone. And pain. Jackson wasn't merely upset. He was devastated. "Please talk to me."

Pushing the remains of his dinner away, he reached for his tea glass. He downed half of it without stopping for breath, then set the glass down with a thump. "How's Tyler?"

"He was a little cross this evening. I think his incision was bothering him. I gave him some Tylenol and read to him until he fell asleep."

Jackson made a sound of self-disgust. "I told him I

would be home in time to play with him before bed-time."

"I told him you wanted to be here, but something came up. You'll have time to play with him tomorrow."

"I'll try."

"Maybe you and your dad could take him for ice cream?" she suggested tentatively. "He always likes hanging out with Daddy and Gampy."

Because she was watching his face, she saw his jaw clench. "Maybe."

She was growing more frustrated with him by the minute. After all his big talk about working as a team during Tyler's hospitalization, now that Jackson was the one in crisis, he refused to open up to her. Once again he had shut her out, relegating her to the silent-partner role she had always chafed against before.

If she were the one in trouble, he would be nagging her to talk to him, demanding to know what he could do to fix everything, because that was what he saw as his duty in their marriage. But that image of protector and defender didn't allow for revealing his own weaknesses, or turning to her for help or even sympathy. He couldn't see that love was a two-way street, and that he was de-liberately putting barriers across the path to his heart.

With a sigh of surrender, she stood. If this was re-ally the marriage Jackson wanted—polite, distant, lonely—then maybe it was time for her to decide once and for all if she was willing to settle for that.

"I'll go check on Tyler," she told him. "Let me know if there's anything else you need."

She didn't expect him to need anything else from her, of course. Or at least nothing that he would admit to.

Twelve

Saying again that she wanted to be close to Tyler, Laurel went to bed in the room upstairs, leaving Jackson sitting in the darkened den pretending to watch a hockey game on TV. She had hung around in the doorway for a few minutes, hoping he might decide to talk to her, after all, but he'd remained silent. Just as Carl had said very little when she'd called him a short while earlier to tell him Jackson was home safely.

Whatever was going on in the Reiss family, it was being made painfully clear to her that she was not a part of it.

She lay awake for a long time, thinking of all the things she had done wrong since the beginning of her marriage, and regretting that it was too late to start over. It was well after midnight when she finally fell asleep.

Less than an hour later, Jackson came to her.

She roused instantly when he sat on the side of the bed. "What is it?" she asked, not quite fully awake yet. "Tyler?"

Jackson put a hand on her shoulder. "Tyler's fine. I just looked in on him."

Shaking off the last remnants of sleep, she blinked him into focus as much as possible in the deeply shadowed room. "What—"

"I'm sorry I woke you."

"That's all right." Rising onto one elbow, she pushed her hair out of her face. "Are you okay?"

He reached out to stroke a fingertip along the line of her jaw. "I missed you in our bed."

She had thought maybe he'd decided he wanted to talk, after all. Now she realized that wasn't at all what he'd had in mind when he had come to her.

He could admit he needed her physically, so why couldn't he acknowledge that she could help him in other ways, as well?

Because this was all she could do for him now, she opened her arms to him. "I miss you, too," she murmured, her words having a deeper, more wistful meaning.

It seemed to be all he needed to hear. He gathered her into his arms and crushed her mouth beneath his.

If there was more than desire in his kiss, a desperation that could not be entirely attributed to lust, this was not the time to confront him about it. Maybe two such stubbornly independent, obsessively self-sufficient people had to learn to communicate the best they could, and maybe words weren't always the only way to share what they were feeling.

Considering the turmoil their emotions were in, she might have expected a heated rush to climax, with much more intensity than finesse. She would have been wrong.

Jackson took his time just kissing her, exploring her mouth from every depth and angle. From soft and sweet to hard and hungry. It had been a long while since he had spent so much time just kissing her, and she was rather surprised by the urgency of her response. Those kisses swept her back to a time when their relationship had been new and exciting, when they had been content to spend hours just holding and enjoying each other. Before pragmatic realities and unreasonable expectations had come between them.

She speared her fingers into his hair, relishing the thickness and softness of it. He gathered her even closer, and she pressed herself against him, savoring his warmth and his strength. She wouldn't change one thing about him physically, she thought, as they drifted into another long, lazy kiss.

She loved so many things about Jackson. His unflinching integrity. His admirable work ethic. His sense of loyalty. Even his devotion to his family, though there were times she thought he went a bit overboard in some respects. When it came right down to it, the only thing she would change about him was how he tried to change *her*.

Eventually his kisses moved from her mouth downward, tracing the line of her arched throat, pausing for a while at the soft, pulsing hollow at the base. He knew she'd always loved to be kissed there. Just as he knew that touching her in that other place always made her gasp softly, as she did now.

When they were together like this, it was just the two of them, lost in each other. If only they could carry that closeness with them back into the real world with its outside demands and intrusions, Laurel thought wistfully. And then Jackson took her right nipple into his mouth, and she could no longer think at all....

Jackson was gone when Laurel woke Sunday morning. He had left a note, so hastily scrawled it barely resembled his handwriting. "Tell Tyler I'm sorry. I'll see him later. Love to you both."

Had he started to sign his name? What might have been a crossed-out *J* was at the bottom of the page.

She checked on Tyler, who was still sleeping, but beginning to stir. He wouldn't sleep much longer. Belting her robe around her, she headed down to the kitchen to start his breakfast. She found the Sunday paper sitting on the table, and a pot of coffee already prepared. A cup of cold coffee sat on the counter. Jackson had apparently poured himself a cup, but hadn't hung around long enough to drink it.

She was going through the motions of a typical weekend morning to avoid thinking about Jackson: the stricken look in his eyes when he'd come home the night before, the way he had sought her out during the night, making love to her until neither of them could move another muscle. She was trying not to think about where he might have gone now, or why he hadn't told her what Donna had said to him.

She was trying not to give in to the despair of wondering if their marriage could survive another blow, especially if it drove him farther away from her.

Why hadn't he talked to her? Why couldn't he see that she was the one person he should have been comfortable talking to about his problems?

When Tyler got up a short while later, he didn't seem particularly surprised that his father wasn't home.

"He go work?" he asked as he finished his breakfast. Though he was too young to know where "work" was, he accepted that his father spent a great deal of time there.

"Yes, he went to work," Laurel fibbed. "But I'm sure he'll be home as soon as he can to spend time with you. In the meantime, would you like to color with the new markers Gammy bought you? You can put stickers on your artwork, too. She brought you a whole new book of stickers."

Always happy to play with art supplies, Tyler settled in his booster seat at the kitchen table to scribble contentedly. It wasn't long before a stack of colorful, sticker-covered works of art littered the kitchen.

Needing something to occupy her own hands, Laurel got out pans and ingredients and started baking. It was something she enjoyed doing occasionally, something her own mother had never attempted, as far as she knew.

Laurel didn't bake because mothers were expected to bake, which would have been Donna's reason, but because she simply enjoyed the measuring and stirring and the delicious aromas that ensued. Not to mention that she liked eating the results, an indulgence she didn't allow herself very often.

There was little pleasure in going through the motions that day. Nor did she imagine that she would have an appetite for sweets, or anything else, until she knew what was going on with Jackson. But baking a fresh banana nut cake gave her something to do besides worry.

When someone tapped on the kitchen door just as the oven timer dinged to let her know the cake was done, her first thought was that Jackson had come home, until she realized he wouldn't need to knock.

She took the cake out and went to open the door to find her father-in-law on the other side. He held a wrapped package in his callused hands and wore a vaguely apologetic look on his weathered face.

"Carl. Please, come in."

"I'm sorry if I'm disturbing anything."

"No, Tyler's just finished playing with his new markers. I was going to let him watch a cartoon before lunch."

"Want to see Scooby-Doo, Gampy?" Tyler offered.

Carl's face softened when he looked at the boy. "No, thanks, Tyler. I need to talk to your mom. But I brought you a present from your grandmother. She would have come herself, but she isn't feeling very well."

Laurel thought for a moment that Tyler was going to be quite spoiled by the time he was fully recuperated from his surgery if he grew accustomed to receiving presents every day, but she decided to worry about that later. She watched as he ripped into the package and exclaimed in pleasure over the toy inside. After instructing him to thank his grandfather, she sent him into the den to play with the new toy.

"Can I get you anything, Carl? I just took a banana nut cake out of the oven. It will be cool enough to frost in a little while."

"I'm not hungry, but I'd take a cup of that coffee if it's still fresh."

"It is. I've been chugging it by the pot today." Motioning him to the table, she filled a mug and carried it to him. She knew he drank his coffee black, and that he liked it strong.

Taking a sip, he nodded approval. "It's good. You always make good coffee."

"It's not that hard. The coffeemaker pretty much does everything on its own."

He grunted. "Doesn't stop some people from ruining it, anyway."

Cradling the mug between his hands, he cleared his throat. "I take it Jay's not here?"

"No. He left early this morning before I woke up. I don't know where he is."

"He's always been one to go off by himself when he's troubled. He's probably walking a beach somewhere. He says he thinks better when there aren't any other distractions around him."

And he would see her as a distraction, rather than a help, Laurel thought sadly. "He wouldn't talk to me. He didn't tell me what happened to upset him."

Carl sighed. "He should have talked to you."

"He didn't." She looked down at her hands as she added in a near whisper, "He rarely does."

"I made some mistakes with Jay," Carl admitted. "I spent so much time teaching him to be strong and independent that I might have overdone it a bit."

Laurel moistened her lips. "I tend to be a bit too independent myself. It's the way I was raised also, though for different reasons."

Carl had been trying to teach Jackson to be a self-sufficient adult, while Laurel's mother was more interested in making her own job as a parent easier. But maybe the end results had been eerily similar.

Clasping her hands in her lap, she leaned forward a bit in her seat. "Carl, will you tell me what happened? I need to know."

Carl shifted uncomfortably in his chair. "That's not really my place, Laurel. I just came by to see if there was anything I can do for you. And I was kind of hoping Jay would be here, and that he would be willing to talk to me."

"Talk to you about what?"

Carl merely shook his head. "He'll tell you. When he's ready."

Laurel wanted to snarl in frustration. In fact, the sound that escaped her came very close to a growl as she leapt to her feet. "Why do I even try? I'm not a part of this family. I never have been."

"Now, Laurel—"

"You know it's true. Donna has disapproved of me since Jackson brought me home and introduced me to her."

"It wasn't that she disapproved. She just didn't have much chance to get to know you before you and Jay got married. And then almost immediately afterward there was Tyler, and all her attention turned to him. She loves that little boy, you know."

"I know. And I would never deprive him of the love of his grandparents. I just wish…"

She didn't actually know what she wished. She wouldn't try to deny that the rift between them was as much her fault as Donna's.

"If it makes you feel any better, Jay isn't talking to me, either," Carl said glumly.

"No, that doesn't make me feel any better at all." She sighed and pushed a lock of hair behind her ear. "But I wouldn't worry about Jackson staying mad at you for long. You and he are so close."

The look that flashed across Carl's usually implacable face startled her. It reminded her all too much of the pain she had seen in her husband's eyes at that same table only a few hours before.

"Carl?"

"I just hope Jay can forgive Donna and me both," he muttered. And then he pushed away from the table. "I'd better go check on my wife. You call me if you need anything, you hear? I'll come right back."

He was trying so hard to hold the family together even in the face of this new crisis—whatever it was. Laurel couldn't help but be touched by his efforts. If her own father had ever been around to offer help and encouragement, maybe it would be easier for her to turn to other people now.

"Jackson's lucky to have you for a father," she said, because Carl seemed to need to hear it.

But maybe that wasn't what he needed to hear at all, because he looked even sadder than before when he patted her arm and let himself out.

Jackson finally showed up late that afternoon. Laurel had just put Tyler down for a nap and was preparing to pace and fret when she glanced up to find Jackson standing in a doorway, looking at her with no expression at all on his face.

"You startled me," she said, placing a hand on her heart. "I didn't hear you come in."

"You were upstairs. I heard you singing to Tyler."

Tyler had requested his favorite song, "You Are My Sunshine." He often begged her to sing it to him before he went to sleep.

"How's he doing?" Jackson glanced at the stairway as he spoke.

"He's fine. He still tires more easily than usual and he doesn't protest when I put him down for naps."

"Which only proves that he isn't quite back to normal."

She nodded. "It won't be long before he screams at the very word *nap* again, I'm sure."

Laurel hoped her own smile didn't look as pathetic as Jackson's. "Yeah," he murmured. "I'm sure he will."

So much for that conversation. They stood awkwardly in the center of the den, searching for something to say and deliberately not looking at each other.

She wanted to ask him where he'd been. She wanted to ask what was going on, and why he hadn't already told her. Most of all, she wanted to ask if there was anything she could do to take the pain from his eyes. It was only her fear that he would turn away from her that kept her from asking any of those questions.

"Are you hungry?" she asked instead, seizing onto a safer topic. "I have some soup. And fresh banana cake."

"I'm not hungry right now."

"Coffee?"

"No, nothing, thanks."

She pushed her hands down the sides of the black slacks she wore with an emerald shirt, nervously dry-ing palms that hadn't really been damp. "Would you like to sit down?"

As soon as the words left her mouth, she winced. She sounded ridiculously like a gracious hostess speaking to a guest in her home.

Jackson must have been thinking very much along the same lines. "Have I really been home that rarely?" he asked in a wry mutter, passing her as he moved toward the couch.

"You work hard. Your boss expects a lot from you."

"And now you're making excuses for me." He sighed, settling wearily into the couch cushions. "I must really look like hell."

"Yes," she said, studying the deep lines around his eyes and mouth. "You do."

He only nodded and shoved a hand through his hair.

She moved to perch on the other end of the couch, half turned to face him, her hands clasped tightly in her lap. She was trying not to ask the questions teeming inside her mind, but she was prepared to listen when he was ready to talk.

His head against the cushion, he closed his eyes, looking so tired and defeated that her heart ached for him. And then he drew a deep breath, sat up straighter, and squared his shoulders. This was his man-in-charge expression, she thought in resignation.

When he spoke, his voice was brisk, steady and unemotional. "I've been doing a lot of thinking during the past couple of days."

"About…?"

"What do you think about moving to Texas?"

She felt her eyes widen. Of all the things he might

have said, she never could have predicted this question. "Why on earth would you want to move to Texas?"

"Remember Kelsey—Mike Kelsey, who used to work with me?"

"Yes. He moved to Houston a couple of years ago, didn't he?"

"Yeah. Anyway, he and I have stayed in touch, he calls or comes by the site when he's in town a couple times a year visiting his folks. He was here last month, and he told me then that the construction business is thriving in that area. He said he was sure he could get me on as a foreman with his company. And he thought there was a chance he and I could strike out on our own within a couple of years, make a decent living in residential construction."

"But…why?"

"Well, you know I haven't been getting on all that well with my boss. And there are excellent medical facilities in Texas for Tyler. I imagine they have need for skilled social workers there, too."

At least he was acknowledging her in some small way. "How long have you been considering this move?"

"I guess it's been in the back of my mind since Kelsey brought it up. Since Tyler got sick, I've been thinking about it more."

Laurel couldn't help but be skeptical. Was this really related to Tyler's surgery—or did it have more to do with whatever Donna had told Jackson yesterday? "But you love Portland. You grew up here."

He shrugged. "Might be nice to live someplace new for a change. Someplace where it doesn't rain all the time," he added with a crooked smile that didn't quite work.

"You've always said you like the rain. And you love the rocky beaches."

"They have beaches in Texas. The Gulf of Mexico is only an hour's drive from Houston."

"Totally different types of beaches than Oregon."

"So we'll try something different. I'm thirty-one years old, and I've never lived more than twenty miles from the hospital where I was born. I think it's past time for me to see a little more of what's out there. It would be good for us, I think. Give us a chance to make a fresh start—just you and me and Tyler."

If he had suggested this move a couple of years ago, maybe even a few months ago, Laurel would have jumped at the chance. As much as she loved working at Children's Connection, the offer of a fresh start in a new place with her husband and son would have been irresistible. But not like this.

"And what about your parents?" she asked evenly.

He lifted an eyebrow, as if in mild surprise at her question. "They'll be fine. We'll visit, of course, but it isn't really necessary for us to live fifteen minutes away from them. They have their lives; we need our own."

She was growing sadder by the moment. As much as Jackson was trying to convince her that this was a move for them, a chance for them to be closer together, she felt even more shut out than before.

She had no doubt that Jackson loved her. Just as she loved him. So why couldn't love be enough to bridge the emotional distance between them?

"Are you planning to tell me the real reason why you want to run to Texas, or am I just supposed to go along with your plans like a good little wife and not ask any questions? And please don't tell me again that you want to move for the scenery or the weather. I would rather you flat out tell me it's none of my business than to brush me off with nonsense."

His eyes narrowed. "I wasn't lying to you. All my reasons for wanting to move are valid ones. And I do think it would be good for the two of us to get away from my—my parents. I would think you'd be the first to agree with that, since you've always resented how prominent a role they've played in our marriage."

She hadn't missed his slight verbal stumble. "What did your mother tell you yesterday, Jackson?"

The length of his hesitation made her wonder if he really was going to tell her it was none of her business. She braced herself for the words, achingly aware that their marriage would be over if he said them.

Maybe the same thought occurred to him. Clearing his throat, he muttered, "She told me that she and Carl have been lying to me my entire life. And it took almost losing our son for them—for my mother—to finally get up the courage to tell me the truth."

Thirteen

"How have your parents been lying to you, Jackson?"

Even as she asked, Laurel still thought it likely that he had just found out he'd been adopted. His reaction seemed a bit extreme, but maybe it was perfectly normal, especially for a man who had always been so close to his parents. She was hardly an expert on how it would feel to be suddenly estranged from her parents, since she had never been particularly close to hers in the first place.

Losing her mother had been a sad experience for her, but mostly because the accident had put an end to any girlhood fantasies Laurel might have harbored of eventually forging a close relationship with Janice. Perhaps as friends, if not a more traditional mother–daughter bond.

Still with that odd lack of expression in his voice, Jackson announced, "Carl Reiss is not my biological father."

For a moment, she thought he had just confirmed her suspicions. But then she realized exactly what he had said. Carl was not his father. "But Donna is your mother?"

"Yeah. Turns out I was the product of a long-time affair between her and an older, married man. She planned to use her pregnancy to force him to leave his wife and kids and marry her, but the scheme backfired when he refused to acknowledge paternity. She married my— She married Carl because she needed someone to take care of her and support her when her lover bailed on her."

Laurel was stunned, as much by the way Jackson had told the story as by the facts he had revealed. He'd made Donna sound like a cold-blooded gold digger. For all of Laurel's criticisms of Donna's annoying quirks, that was a far different image than she had ever had of Jackson's mother.

"She must have been very young," she offered tentatively, quickly doing the math. Twenty-one. Very young for some people, though Laurel had been on her own for years by that age.

"I think she knew what she was doing. From what she told me, she had her eyes on the guy's bank account from the start."

"Well, obviously she's changed in the past thirty-one years. Donna likes nice things, but she hardly lives a lavish lifestyle. She brags about being a bargain shopper, for heaven's sake. You've said yourself that she can stretch a penny as if it were made of rubber."

He had held that up as another one of his mother's many virtues, actually, boasting about how content she had always been with her husband's comfortable, working-class income. Usually that observation came in the middle of one of his complaints about Laurel's work obligations.

"So she settled for a man with less money," Jackson muttered with a shrug. "But she never had to work and never lacked for anything she really wanted, so I guess she figures she made out okay, after all."

"I don't think she would agree that she merely settled. She's always seemed very happy to me."

"Yeah, well, you can't always tell with her, can you?"

There was still anger beneath the sarcasm, and pain. All of which she understood. Jackson had a right to be angry that he'd been deceived for so long—as long as he kept his anger in perspective and didn't do anything he would regret. Like packing up and moving to Texas, she added wryly.

The one person he hadn't really discussed yet was Carl. Laurel suspected that was the deepest cut of all, as far as Jackson was concerned. He quite simply adored Carl Reiss. He had spent his entire life trying to learn from him, to be like him. How many times had she heard him laughingly proclaim himself to be just like his dad? He'd even commented a time or two that he thought Tyler had Carl's eyes.

Now his world had shifted. His way of looking at Carl, his image of himself as Carl's son, even his perception of his own son as the youngest in a long line of Reiss men—all of that had changed.

"Your dad is worried about you," she said, choosing her words deliberately. "He wants you to talk to him."

"Where was he yesterday, when Mom told me the truth?"

"He thought it best for her to be the one to tell you. And maybe he was worried about how you would react. You know how much he loves you, Jackson. He's probably scared half to death about the way you feel about him now."

Jackson looked down at his hands, and Laurel suspected that he didn't know the answer to that himself.

"You know you still love Carl, and that he loves you," she said by way of reminder. "You're angry with him right now, and that's only natural, but it will get better."

She didn't know whether to interpret his grunt as agreement with her words or the opposite, but she could tell he wasn't feeling any better. She searched her mind for something, anything, to say to help him through this.

The telephone rang before she came up with anything. She moved to answer it, but Jackson detained her by laying a hand on her leg. "Let the machine get it."

She looked at him in question. "It could be important."

"You know it's probably my mother. I'm not ready to talk to her yet."

"It could be your dad."

A muscle twitched in his jaw. "I don't want to talk to anyone right now."

She nodded. The call could be for her, of course, but Jackson was probably right about the caller's identity.

And she didn't really want to talk to Donna, either. For one thing, she wouldn't know how to answer if either Donna or Carl asked how Jackson was doing.

Getting him to talk about this was like pulling teeth, but she decided to keep prodding him. Maybe if he could just express his feelings, it would ease some of his pain. "Did your mother tell you anything else?"

Jackson reached up to rub his right temple, as if to soothe an ache there. "Yeah. She told me the name of my biological father. Apparently she's been in touch with him and confirmed that Tyler's heart condition did come from his genes."

Which only gave Jackson another reason to resent the man, Laurel thought sympathetically. "Is it anyone you know?"

"Not personally. I've heard the name. I'm sure you have, too. According to my mother, her rich boyfriend was Jack Crosby."

That made her eyes widen. "Well, of course I've heard of Jack Crosby."

"Jack." His upper lip curled as he said the name. "My mother must have thought it was very clever of her to name me after him."

Laurel winced. "I'm sure she had her reasons."

"Yeah. She told me she was still mad enough when I was born to name me that as a dig at Crosby. Heck of a reason to choose a name for your son, isn't it?" He shook his head in disgust.

It did seem like a rather cold thing to do, especially when another man had volunteered to be a father to her boy. "She was young," she said lamely, having no other excuse for Donna.

"Quit saying that, okay? She was old enough to try to bust up a family and then to find someone else to support her. She knew what she was doing."

She started to try again to defend his mother, maybe to remind him that everyone made mistakes—some worse than others, of course—but she decided to wait until he'd cooled down a bit more. Though he had a temper, Jackson was ultimately a reasonable man to whom family meant everything. He would come around eventually.

"Apparently now he wants to meet me."

She followed the shift of topic with an effort. "Jack Crosby, you mean?"

He nodded.

"How do you feel about that?"

"Uninterested," he answered succinctly.

"He has several other grown children, doesn't he? Three or four, I think. They're your half-siblings, Jackson."

"They're strangers. The fact that we share some DNA doesn't make us family."

"No, but—"

"I doubt that they'd be any more interested in meeting me. How do you think it would make them feel to find out that their father was screwing around with a waitress while he was married to their mother? Not to mention they would probably assume I'd make a claim for part of their inheritance."

Laurel hadn't even thought of that. Jack Crosby was a multimillionaire. For that matter, Jackson probably *did* have a legal claim to an inheritance, even though she knew her stubbornly proud husband would reject the very suggestion. "It's up to you whether you meet Jack Crosby, of course. But maybe it isn't such a bad idea. Maybe you can resolve all this easier in your mind if you meet everyone involved."

He shot her a heated glare. "Suddenly you want to get involved with your in-laws? I guess a few million dollars makes the idea a bit more appealing, huh?"

He had spoken rashly, probably lashing out more at her suggestion than at her personally. But it still hurt. Badly.

She rose stiffly, wrapping her arms around her middle. "That was unfair. You're angry with your parents, and I can understand that. But I will not allow you to take that anger out on me. Not when I'm only trying to help you."

"Look, I'm sorry. I just—I really don't want to talk about this anymore."

"Fine." She turned toward the doorway. "I'll go check on Tyler."

Okay, maybe he hadn't handled that very well.

Jackson sighed deeply. He might as well be honest. He'd botched the conversation with Laurel big-time.

He shouldn't have sprung the Texas suggestion on her so abruptly. It was just that it seemed like a good idea at the time. Still did, for that matter. He'd thought Laurel would be more intrigued by the idea of moving so far away from his parents.

He'd put off telling her about his parentage as long as he could. It hadn't been something he'd looked forward to. He had told himself that he would be cool and dispassionate when he told her. That he would let none of his tumultuous emotions show in either his voice or his expression. He wanted her to know that he was a strong, mature adult who could handle whatever came at him. Just like his—

Like Carl, he thought with the hollow ache that had been inside him ever since he had left his mother's house the day before.

It was bad enough that he had learned things about his mother that had completely shaken his image of the woman he had thought he knew so well. But to find out that Carl wasn't really his father... Well, that had been almost too much to bear.

He buried his face in his hands. He wished he hadn't lashed out at Laurel when she'd suggested that he might want to meet Jack Crosby. He shouldn't have practically accused her of being a gold digger.

Just because his mother had once coveted Crosby's money didn't mean Laurel felt the same way. He didn't blame Laurel for being angry, especially since they'd been struggling for so long to learn to communicate.

If he kept going like this, he was going to end up completely alone. For a man who had taken such pride in his family only a couple of weeks earlier, that was hard even to contemplate.

To say that Laurel was having a difficult day would have been a massive understatement. Tyler woke up from his nap sore and cranky, maybe sensing the undercurrents of tension in his home. Jackson brooded in a corner of the den, pretending to watch golf on TV—and he didn't even like golf. He made an occasional effort to pay attention to his son, but Tyler was in a mood to whine and cling to his mommy.

Torn between them, feeling as if they both needed something from her she didn't know how to offer, Laurel went about her usual household chores as best as she could with Tyler practically clinging to her legs. It was all she knew to do to make everything appear normal and reassuring for Tyler, when everything was so obviously *not* normal.

She served an early dinner that no one ate. Passed out cookies that were nibbled then abandoned. Started conversations with Jackson that quickly fizzled into silence. Tried playing games that didn't hold Tyler's interest.

At her wit's end, she finally gave Tyler some pain relievers for his discomfort, then settled into a rocking chair with him and his stuffed penguin in her lap. Three choruses of "You Are My Sunshine" later, he was sound asleep.

"Is he okay?" Jackson leaned against the doorway of Tyler's room, watching her gently rock their child. She didn't know how long he had been there, since he'd made no sound until he spoke.

Though she was still annoyed with him over that crack about her supposed interest in his biological father's money, she tried to keep her quiet tone cordial. "His incision is bothering him some. And he still tires too easily. I was warned to expect those things, but he gets stronger every day."

"Is there anything I can do?"

She shook her head. "I was just about to put him to bed. I think he's out for the night."

Jackson glanced at his watch. "It's barely eight o'clock."

"His usual bedtime is eight-thirty," she reminded him. She supposed he'd forgotten since he was so rarely home before nine. "He needs about ten hours of sleep a night at this stage."

"Here." He moved away from the doorway. "Let me carry him to the bed for you."

Tyler barely stirred during the transfer from Laurel's arms to Jackson's. "Daddy?" he mumbled without opening his eyes.

"Just putting you into bed, sport."

"'Kay."

Jackson was smiling a little when he bent to deposit the boy onto his pillows. It was the first time Laurel had seen him smile all day.

She moved to the other side of the bed to tuck Tyler in, settling Angus into the crook of his arm. "Good night, sweetie," she whispered, kissing his soft cheek.

His eyes still closed, Tyler breathed, "Night, Mommy."

He was asleep again before she straightened up.

She and Jackson both stood for several long minutes on opposite sides of the bed, gazing down at their son. And then their eyes lifted, and they stared, instead, at each other.

"He's still the best part of me," Jackson murmured.

"The best part of us both."

"Someday I'll have to tell him the truth about his heritage."

She nodded. "Yes. He'll need to know his complete medical history."

Jackson pushed a hand through his hair. Though he still spoke very quietly, there was a great deal of emotion roiling in his voice when he said, "I was always so proud to be a Reiss. I wanted Tyler to share that pride."

She swallowed around a hard lump in her throat. "He will. He *does*. You're still Carl Reiss's son, and this is his grandson. That hasn't changed."

"Hasn't it?" He looked away from her. "I need to go by the office to pick up some paperwork for tomorrow. I won't be gone long."

He was running again. From her this time, probably because he was afraid she saw too well what he was going through.

She was sure he told himself that he just needed time to shore up his emotional barricades. To make sure he had all signs of vulnerability—which he would consider weakness—hidden.

A real man dealt with his own problems, after all. Real men *gave* emotional support. They never asked for it for themselves. They shouldn't need to, at least according to the teachings of strong and stoic Carl Reiss. The only father Jackson had ever known.

"What should I say if your parents call?"

"Just tell them…tell them I'll talk to them later," he said, moving toward the door.

He paused just before he stepped out of the room. "Laurel?"

"Yes?"

"About what I said earlier… I'm sorry. It was a stupid remark, and I know it wasn't true. It's long past time for me to stop trying to compare you to my mother. It won't happen again."

Laurel sighed as she watched him leave without giving her a chance to respond. She hadn't expected the apology, though she deserved it. She certainly hadn't expected him to admit that he had unfairly compared her to his mother, and on more than this one occasion.

Thinking about the things he had said, and the look on his face when he had spoken, she returned to the rocker to watch her son sleep for a while longer.

Carl didn't call. He came by. Not half an hour after Jackson left, Carl showed up at the back door, as was his habit. "I didn't think anyone would answer the phone if I called," he admitted.

"Come in."

He stepped past her, searching her face as he did so. "You okay?"

"I'm fine. How is Donna?"

"She's a mess," he answered flatly. "Is Jay here?"

"No. He went to his office for a little while. He was getting too restless sitting here thinking."

Carl nodded his understanding. "I never can just sit around the house much, either. I've been trying to stay with Donna this weekend, but I just have to get out every once in a while. That's why I came over here, to see if everything's okay."

"Want some coffee?"

"No, thanks. I think I've already had a couple of pots today."

"At least sit down."

He pulled out a chair at the kitchen table and sank into it. "I guess Jay's told you everything by now."

"He gave me the abridged version, I think. But I know the basic facts."

"How's Jay holding up?"

She hesitated a moment before answering. And then she decided to be candid. "He's hurting. He's angry. He's confused about who he is and how he feels about what he's learned."

"He's mad that we didn't tell him earlier. I guess I don't blame him about that. I always— Well…"

"You wanted to tell him sooner?"

Carl looked torn for a moment between protecting his wife and being honest. "Donna just never thought the time was right. By the time Jay was old enough to understand, we'd settled into such a comfortable family routine that it seemed a shame to risk messing it up. He was such a good kid, didn't get into much of that teen rebellion everyone worries about with their boys. She—we didn't want to do anything that would make him turn against us."

"Surely you knew the truth would come out someday."

"Well, no. I guess we were being unrealistic, but we thought there was a good chance he would never have to know the whole story."

"I hope he can come to understand that you were doing what you thought best for him. It's just— Well, you know Jackson. He hates being lied to."

Carl took offense at that. He lifted his chin, his sun-lined eyes narrowing more than usual. "As far as I'm concerned, I never lied to him. I married his mama before he was born. I was there at the hospital to welcome him when he came out. I held him in my arms when he wasn't fifteen minutes old, and I told him then that I was his daddy, and that I would give my life for him if necessary. I meant every word of it."

Laurel and Carl had probably talked more in the last week than in the last four years. She had always respected him, but the better she got to know him, the fonder she became of him.

Sure, he was part of the reason Jackson was so reluctant to show his feelings, and most of the gender-role beliefs Carl had passed on were downright archaic, but he was a good man. She believed without doubt that he loved his wife, son and grandson, and that he really would lay down his life for any one of them. She knew he could not have loved Jackson any more had his own blood run through Jackson's veins.

"I'll talk to him some more, Carl," she promised. And then amended, "Well, I'll try. He isn't an easy man to talk to, you know."

Carl blew out a short breath. "Guess he's a lot like me in that respect."

"Yes," she said gently, impulsively reaching out to lay her hand over his. "He's just like his dad."

Carl's throat worked, and for just a moment, she thought she saw a quick sheen of what might have been tears in his weathered eyes. He masked the emotions immediately, patting her hand and making an effort to smile a little. "You're a nice woman, Laurel. Good heart. Helping other people isn't just your job, it's your nature."

Now it was her time to blink back tears. Perhaps she was tired, or overstressed, but Carl's words touched her to the very core. This was the type of approval she had once craved from her own father.

Because he was still Carl, and still uncomfortable with expressing such emotions, he didn't give her a chance to say anything. Rising abruptly, he pushed his chair back beneath the table. "I think I'd better go before Jay gets back. Tell him… Well, just tell him I dropped by, okay?"

She knew there were many more things he wanted to say, but didn't know how. "I'll tell him."

He nodded, then let himself out.

Gazing after him, Laurel told herself that Jackson was still very much like his dad—and no matter who his biological father was, his dad would always be Carl Reiss.

Fourteen

Jackson was home before ten. Laurel waited for him in the den, where she had been trying to read a mystery that would have held her attention at any other time. She closed the book and set it aside when he came in. "You missed your dad again."

"Came by kind of late, didn't he?"

"He's worried about you."

Jackson shrugged and dropped into an armchair. "No need for him to be."

"Maybe you'd like to give him a call? I'm sure he hasn't gone to bed yet."

"Not tonight. I'll talk to him another time."

"You should talk to him soon, Jackson. He misses you."

"I said I will. Later."

"And your mother? She's waiting to hear from you, too."

"Yeah. Later. So, have you given any more thought to me looking into that job in Texas? Because I was thinking I could take a few days off in a couple of weeks, when Tyler's feeling better, and fly out there to talk to some people. If the job looks as good as Kelsey made it sound, we could start looking at houses and school districts there."

He must have read some of her thoughts in her expression. "This really isn't as impulsive as it sounds," he said, his tone defensive. "I've been thinking about it ever since Kelsey was here last month. The only reason I didn't mention it before was that we were both so busy before Tyler's surgery that we hardly had time to talk. Kelsey said he doesn't work the crazy hours I do here. He's pretty much eight to ten hours a day, rarely more than five days a week. You and Tyler and I would have more time together. Isn't that what you've wanted?"

"It is," she admitted. "I think we need to spend more time together as a family. But it has to be for the right reasons, Jackson. Moving there to escape our problems here won't work. People carry their emotional baggage everywhere they go, and I don't like the thought of leaving our friends and family here only to end up unhappy and estranged in Texas."

"There's no reason to think that will happen," he said a bit stiffly. "Our only real problems here have been my working hours—well, and sometimes yours, and the fact that you've resented my parents interfering so often in our affairs. That can't happen if we live so far away from them."

Laurel gave a sigh of exasperation. Did Jackson really believe he had just concisely summed up their marital problems in a couple of sentences? If he did, then maybe they were in worse trouble than she had even imagined.

"You know what I was thinking about when I drove home from the office tonight?" he asked unexpectedly.

"No. What?"

"Our honeymoon."

That took her by surprise, since it seemed so unconnected to anything else they had been discussing. "Hawaii?"

"Yeah. I think that's the last time we spent more than a full day together. Tyler was born less than a year later, and we both got caught up in him and in our jobs. Mom saw Tyler as a way to solve her empty-nest syndrome, so she started spending more and more time here. And I spent too many weekends when I wasn't working fishing with—with Dad, instead of being with you and Tyler."

He still couldn't mention Carl without hesitating, she thought with a pang of sympathy.

He continued quickly, as if hoping she hadn't noticed. "Anyway, for some reason I started thinking about our honeymoon today. We had a lot of fun that week, didn't we?"

It had been nonstop fun from beginning to end. They had laughed and played like two irresponsible kids, and Laurel had been so naively certain their marriage would continue just that way. Fun. Passionate. Carefree.

Watching him interact with his parents afterward had altered her rather fanciful illusion that it was just the two of them against the world. Having a helpless infant placed in her arms only a few months later had forever changed her carefree view of life and marriage. Sitting alone in her house with a crying baby in her arms and a case of postpartum depression draining all of her energy and enthusiasm, waiting for her husband to make an occasional appearance from work, had taken away the rest of her expectations for a fairy-tale life.

But she still remembered every minute of that honeymoon. "Yes. It was fun."

"Remember the big luau, when those hula dancers pulled you onto the stage and had you dance with them?"

Echoes of music and laughter filled her mind as she nodded. "Of course."

"I remember watching you up there. You were so beautiful. You looked as though you were having such a good time. You moved as gracefully as any of the native dancers, though you didn't know the steps. I remember thinking that I was the luckiest guy in the world, and that every man at that luau must be envying me."

A single tear escaped to slide down her right cheek. She reached up to wipe it away. She wasn't the only one who had found marriage to be different than she had expected, she reminded herself. Motherhood had changed her drastically from the woman Jackson had proposed to.

She had worked so hard before to be the life of the party, someone others gravitated to for fun and laughter. She had spent so much of her childhood alone that she'd deliberately surrounded herself with people after her mother died.

Everything had changed for her the day she learned she was pregnant. She had been stunned—and then determined not to fail at the most important role of her life. Overwhelmed by fear and responsibility and an almost crippling lack of confidence in her mothering abilities, she had put all of her energy into taking care of Tyler. What little she'd had left had been directed into the job that had been her one refuge from fear and insecurity. That hadn't left much of anything for Jackson.

"I had such a good time at that luau," she murmured. "Everything seemed so perfect. The two of us on an island in paradise. Together all day every day, with no more pressing responsibilities than to find something to eat occasionally."

"Everything changed when we came home to find ourselves expecting a baby, didn't it? I guess neither of us was really prepared for that."

"It scared me to my toenails," she admitted, possibly for the first time aloud. "I knew so little about being a mother. I felt confident about finding parents for other babies, but I had absolutely no confidence in my own abilities. I wasn't even sure then that I would approve myself as an adoptive parent."

"Funny," he said, though there was no humor in his expression, "I was just as insecure about my role as a father. You were afraid that having no role model would be a problem for you, but my dilemma was somewhat the opposite. I didn't think I could ever be the same kind of dad I had. I tried so hard to be just like him," he added in a rough murmur.

Laurel swallowed, then suggested tentatively, "And maybe you tried a little too hard to encourage me to be just like your mother? Your own upbringing was so perfect, in your opinion, that you tried to duplicate it almost exactly for Tyler."

"I didn't—" he began with a hint of irritation. And then he stopped himself, thought a moment, then sighed deeply. "I don't know. Maybe."

Since they were being so honest, for a change, Laurel risked one more confession. "I knew I could never be like Donna. And I knew that trying to make myself into her would lead to disaster. I decided I had to be myself—and that I would have to let you go if you came to the conclusion that I wasn't what you wanted. I thought that was exactly what you *had* decided when you started spending more and more time away from me."

"That's what I'm trying to tell you," he murmured. "You *are* exactly what I want. I've been doing a lot of thinking during the past couple of days, about many things. I've got to admit that it hurts to feel estranged from my parents, but I can deal with that. Eventually. But the past couple of years I've felt that I was losing you—and that's a loss I don't want to have to face.

"When I realized how close we came to losing our son, I fully understood that you and Tyler are my whole world. Maybe I haven't told you enough. Hell, I know I haven't. I've tried to show you, and I guess I wasn't too good at that, either. But it's true. You're the one I want—the one I've always wanted."

He cleared his throat, then continued when she sat silently trying to digest his words. "You're an amazing mother, Laurel. Tyler is a happy, well-adjusted kid, and you've made him that way. You've pursued your own life, yes, but in your case, that seems to make you an even better mother. I watched your co-workers and your clients this past week, and I saw how much they respect you and how grateful they are for the work you do. I realized that I've been incredibly selfish trying to keep you from doing that work. *I'm* the one who got so caught up in trying to be the great provider that I neglected the very family I was trying to provide for."

The self-recrimination in his voice took her aback. For some reason, she hadn't truly comprehended that Jackson had been as afraid of parenthood as she had been. That he'd felt the crushing weight of responsibility, just as she had, and that he had dealt with it the only way he had known how—by working even harder.

They really should have talked about these feelings sooner, she thought regretfully. The last few years could have been much different if they had been more open with their feelings from the start.

She said something along those lines to Jackson, adding, "I suppose I was afraid to let you know how scared I was. I thought you would think less of me if you knew what a mess I was inside."

His voice was gruff when he replied, "I guess I felt the same way. I'd been taught that men don't let their fear show. That their actions should speak louder than their words. Maybe that works for my parents, but it isn't right for us. We have to learn to talk, Laurel. I need to know when you're afraid or unhappy or worried, and I have to learn to tell you how I feel. Both of us need to stop being so damned strong and independent and learn to be half of a true partnership."

"That's all I've ever wanted," she whispered, wiping

her eyes again. She had never let Jackson see her cry. Maybe that, too, had been her way of holding him at an emotional distance.

His eyes were dark with emotion when he leaned toward her and spoke with a sincerity she could not have mistaken. "I have never doubted that I loved you. Maybe there were times when I wondered if we married too quickly—"

"We probably did," she cut in ruefully. "It was all such a crazy, romantic whirlwind that we didn't have a chance to work out all of the practical details beforehand."

"And then we let parenthood, and other family issues, interfere."

"We've both made mistakes," she said firmly. "We came from very different backgrounds and had different expectations, and that was bound to cause problems. We'll undoubtedly have more problems and make more mistakes in the future. But I love you, too, Jackson. I have from the night we met. We have a lot going for us, including an absolutely perfect little boy who has been given a second chance at growing up strong and healthy. I'm willing to start over if you are."

"In Texas?"

She kept her voice even. "If that's where we decide to go. I just want to make sure that we would be moving there for the right reasons."

Jackson stood and held out a hand to her. She placed hers in it and allowed him to draw her to her feet.

"Remember what we did after the luau?" he asked, sliding his arms around her. "We went back to our room, and we danced together—"

She locked her arms around his neck, gazing up at the man whose sexy smile had made her knees go weak that night. It still did, she discovered as she leaned against him. "I remember."

His mouth covering hers, he moved his feet in a slow, seductive dance that she followed easily. And then he swept her into his arms and headed for their bedroom.

Smiling shakily, Laurel tucked her head into the crook of his neck and remembered that their dance hadn't lasted very long that other night, either. But the spectacular lovemaking that had followed…

She sighed in anticipation.

The bedroom was dark enough that Laurel could almost imagine she was back in the honeymoon suite in Hawaii. A faint scent of the tropical scented potpourri she kept in a glass dish on the nightstand added to that illusion, carrying her back to the time when she and Jackson had been giddy newlyweds, so feverishly in love that they both thought they would explode with it.

The years since that honeymoon faded away as Jackson helped her out of her clothes, punctuating each movement with kisses and caresses. For the first time in much too long, she felt young and sexy again, unconcerned with the faint, lingering marks of pregnancy or any of the other slight changes that time had wrought in either of them. Jackson was as attractive to her now as he had ever been, and he left her in no doubt that he felt the same about her.

Though he knew every inch of her body, he took his time exploring her again, as if for the first time. She stripped away his shirt and pants, wanting the freedom to do the same with him.

The barriers between them during these past months had been emotional rather than physical, but it felt almost as if she were really touching him again for the first time since that honeymoon. Baring her emotions to him had stripped her of other inhibitions, as well, so that she was able to give herself fully to their lovemaking now. Judging from the wonder in his touches and the excited murmurs he made as they kissed and touched, he must have felt much the same way.

He laid her gently on the bed, leaning over her to nuzzle her breasts with his lips and his tongue. Her nipples were swollen and aching by the time he moved on, her hips moving restlessly on the bed as she urged him to her. She reached down to touch him intimately, finding him so fiercely aroused that she marveled at his self-control. Still he took his time, his fingers sliding between her legs to stroke her almost to the edge of madness before he settled on top of her.

Digging her fingertips into his damp shoulders, she arched upward. "Jackson," she whispered, and her tone was a hoarse mixture of demand and pleading.

"I love you," he murmured, just before thrusting so deeply into her that she thought he touched her very soul.

She wanted to tell him that she loved him, too, but an explosion of sensation robbed her of the ability to speak. Instead, she concentrated on giving him a thorough demonstration of exactly how she felt about him.

Jackson seemed unusually reluctant to leave for work the next morning. He lingered over breakfast, teasing with Tyler and giving Laurel looks that brought a warm flush to her cheeks. And then he sighed and reached for the case that held the paperwork he would need at the site that day. "I guess I'd better go."

"Bye, Daddy."

Jackson lightly squeezed his son's shoulder. "What are your plans for the day, sport?"

"Mommy and I are going to the grocery store." He looked as excited as if he'd said they were going to a carnival, Laurel thought indulgently. Poor child probably was looking forward to going someplace that wasn't a hospital.

"It's okay to take him out?" Jackson asked, looking a bit concerned.

"As long as we aren't out for long. I won't let him get too close to anyone who might have a cold or virus."

"Make him wash his hands when he gets home."

She knew that of course, but didn't bother to point it out. Jackson needed to feel useful, needed to feel that he was making a contribution. It was a part of his nature that would never change. "I will."

He gave her a half smile that told her he was well aware she hadn't needed his advice, but was pleased she had acknowledged it. And then he left for work, promising to be home as early as he could. For once, Laurel believed that he really would make that effort.

She and Tyler made the planned trip to the grocery store, stopping for milkshakes on the way home. She was both delighted and relieved to note that the outing didn't seem to tire him overly much. He hadn't regained full strength yet, but he was well on his way, she thought in satisfaction.

Tyler took a short nap after the outing, during which

Laurel did some laundry and made a few calls—one of them to set up a meeting with Leslie Logan's daughter and new son-in-law the following week in her home. She would have to visit their home, as well, but the preliminary interview could take place here, she decided. As fond as she was of Leslie, she would grant no special favors to her daughter, other than agreeing to doing these interviews during her leave of absence, of course.

She hoped the uncomfortable feelings she'd gotten during her first meeting with Bridget and Sam would be assuaged when she spoke to them at length.

Tyler woke in a good mood. He and Laurel built a castle with plastic interlocking blocks, and then she watched indulgently as he noisily knocked the castle down. Leaving him to entertain himself for a while, she went down to the kitchen to prepare a chicken casserole for dinner. It should be ready by the time Jackson arrived home, she thought, especially if he kept his word about coming home at a normal hour.

The front doorbell rang, summoning her from the kitchen. Wiping her hands on a paper towel, she went to answer it, half expecting to find a neighbor or a delivery driver on the doorstep. Instead, she found her in-laws—both of them this time.

Laurel had always thought Donna Reiss looked young for her fifty-two years. Now she looked a good ten years older. She had obviously been crying; her eyes were red and swollen. She wore little makeup, and the fine lines around her eyes and mouth were more pronounced than usual. Laurel would be surprised if Donna had slept since Jackson had left her house Saturday afternoon.

With her hand to her throat, Donna said in a wavering voice, "I know you probably don't want to see me, but please let me see Tyler. Just for a little while."

Laurel bit back a sigh in response to her mother-in-law's melodrama. "Donna, you will always be welcome in this house," she said firmly, moving out of the doorway to motion them inside. "You're Tyler's grandmother and he adores you. I would never deprive him or you of that relationship."

"See, Donna?" Carl nodded in satisfaction. "I told you Laurel wasn't going to try to keep you from Tyler. She's worked herself into a state," he added to Laurel. "I thought the best way to ease her mind was just to bring her over and let you reassure her. Guess we should have called, but I didn't give her a chance to dial. I told her to just get in the car and we were coming over."

"Tyler's playing in his room. Can I get either of you anything before I call him down?"

"No. Thank you," Donna added as an afterthought. "I just want to see him."

"I'll go get him." Laurel hesitated a moment, then added, "He doesn't know there have been any problems within the family, of course. I would rather not upset him."

"I wouldn't dream of upsetting him," Donna replied, lifting her chin and making a visible effort to restore her usual equanimity. "Surely you know that."

"I know you love him." Laurel spoke a bit more gently this time, touched despite herself by the pain in Donna's eyes. "He's lucky to have a close relationship with his grandparents. I never knew mine, and I regret that to this day."

Donna bit her lip. "Thank you, Laurel."

From behind his wife's back, Carl gave Laurel an unusually sweet smile of gratitude.

Telling them to have a seat in the den, Laurel headed for the stairs. Had Donna really believed she would try to keep her away from Tyler? Perhaps Donna had thought Laurel would take pleasure in Jackson's temporary estrangement from his mother—and she was sure it would be temporary. But if Donna thought Laurel would take advantage of a crisis to split up a family, then she really didn't know her well at all.

She had never wanted to break up the Reiss family, she realized as she stood outside Tyler's bedroom. She had simply wanted to be accepted as one of them. And it had been as much her fault as theirs that it had never worked out quite that way. Maybe she had subconsciously pushed them away from the start because she was so accustomed to rejection by family that she'd been trying to protect herself from being hurt again.

She had often blamed Jackson for the rift, telling herself that his impossible comparisons between her and his mother kept Laurel from wanting to be close to the woman. That had been unfair, she saw now. She had used Jackson's closeness to his family as an excuse—perhaps because she had so desperately envied that closeness.

Now that his family was threatened, she couldn't bear the thought of breaking those ties. For Jackson's sake. For Tyler's. And for her own last chance at belonging to a supportive, loving extended family who accepted each other for who they are, without trying to change them or have them prove their worthiness of love.

Maybe they could be that kind of family, after all, she thought with a rush of hope. Once Jackson got over his hurt and accepted that his mother had made mistakes, maybe they could all forgive Laurel for the mistakes she had made in holding them at arm's length for so long. And maybe she and Donna could finally learn to see each other as friends, and not rivals for the affections of Jackson and Tyler.

But they had a way to go before they could reach that idealized goal, she reminded herself, still the experience-scarred pessimist. Jackson had to reconcile with his parents before Laurel could have the chance to do so herself.

Jackson arrived home even earlier than Laurel expected. His parents were still playing in the den with Tyler, and she had just taken dinner out of the oven when Jackson came into the kitchen from the garage.

"I saw the truck outside," he said by way of greeting. "Is he here?"

"Yes, your father is here," Laurel replied, emphasizing the relationship. "And so is your mother. She wanted to see Tyler, so Carl brought her over. Can you believe she was afraid I wouldn't let her in to see her grandson?"

Without saying anything, Jackson set his briefcase on the counter.

Laurel lifted an eyebrow. "Jackson? You wouldn't expect me to turn them away, would you?"

"No, of course not." He pushed a hand through his hair. "Did they say how much longer they plan to stay?"

"I'm going to ask them to stay for dinner. I made plenty for everyone."

A frown drew his eyebrows downward. "Oh."

She sighed and placed her hands on her hips as she faced him. "This is ridiculous. You can't keep avoiding them. I don't care what happened more than thirty years ago, Carl and Donna Reiss are your parents. You love them, they love you, and nothing will ever change that, no matter what. Now would you please stop sulking and deal with this like the man Carl raised you to be?"

Carl spoke from behind her before Jackson had a chance to defend himself. "In case I haven't mentioned it before, I wholeheartedly approve of the woman you married, Jay."

Fifteen

Laurel turned. Carl leaned against the doorjamb, his arms crossed over his sturdy chest and a bland look on his face that was probably intended to mask his uncertainty as he searched Jackson's expression.

She glanced back at Jackson, seeing a similar anxiety reflected in his eyes when he looked at her. Then he said to Carl, "I don't think any of us have made it clear enough during the past few years that Laurel deserves our admiration and respect."

Laurel's face warmed in embarrassment, but Carl merely nodded his agreement with Jackson's comment. "No, we haven't. We seem to have a problem with communication in our family. We don't talk enough about important things. We don't tell each other often enough how we feel about each other. Heck, when I tried to tell you at the hospital how proud I am of you, you thought I must be dying."

Laurel thought that must have been a very interesting conversation. She would have left them to talk alone now, but Carl still blocked the doorway. Staying as inconspicuous as possible, she stood very still as Jackson said, "I shouldn't have had to find out like this."

"No, son, you shouldn't have," Carl replied heavily. "I'm real sorry for that, and so is your mother. We hope you can forgive us someday, and that you'll understand that we did the best we knew how at the time."

"Do you really think we can go on as if nothing at all has changed?" Jackson asked. "Mom said this guy wants to meet me now that he knows about me. What am I supposed to do about that?"

Carl shrugged, then spoke with his usual bluntness. "Nothing *has* changed. As Laurel just pointed out, we have thirty-one years of history between us. You are my son, and I wouldn't love you one bit more if we had the same blood type or DNA. Now, as it happens, there's another man who does share those things with you. If you want to meet him and your half siblings, that's up to you. Your mother doesn't want you to have anything to do with them, but I told her she needs to leave that to you. You've got a right to know them if you want to. Doesn't mean anything has to change between you and your mother and me."

Laurel held her breath as she waited for Jackson to respond. He took his time about it. After all, Carl had conveyed quite a lot in typically few words.

Finally, Jackson nodded and straightened away from the counter where he had been leaning. Even if it were due more to imitation than inheritance, Laurel thought his expression looked very much like Carl's when he said, "For the past three years, I've tried to be the kind of father to Tyler that you were to me. Maybe I need to change a few things, like not working so many hours and being more willing to talk about important things, but I still think I couldn't have had a better role model. I just hope someday Tyler feels about me the way I do about you."

Carl swallowed hard, then reached out to lightly punch Jackson's arm. His version of a hug, Laurel thought wryly. "We're straight, then?"

Maybe it wouldn't be quite as easy as Carl obviously hoped, but Jackson seemed to know Carl needed reassurance. "Yeah, Dad. We're straight."

"And your mother? Are you going to forgive her, too?"

Jackson hesitated. "I can't deny that I've had a hard time reconciling what she told me with the woman I've always believed her to be."

"She's exactly the woman you thought she was." Carl spoke with a touch of heat now, obviously ready to defend his wife. "She made some mistakes when she was a kid—hell, I made more than a few, myself—but she's been a damned good wife to me and mother to you. Excuse my language, Laurel."

She nodded, faintly amused by yet another display of Carl's old-fashioned gallantry.

"Anyway, I never blamed Donna for falling for Jack Crosby. The guy's smooth as satin, and she wasn't the only young woman he deceived, I'm sure. I was glad to be there when she needed me, and in return she's given me thirty-one years of happy marriage. And don't you go doubting that she loves either of us, Jay. It didn't take long for me to teach her the difference between a slick operator and a real man."

This time Laurel had to suppress a smile. As usual, Carl had stated his opinions without arrogance or tact. Laurel thought it must be nice to be so confident in one's beliefs.

"Laurel?" Donna stepped into the doorway, looking from one of them to the other as if trying to guess what they had been talking about. Though she continued speaking to Laurel, her gaze remained on her son's face. "Tyler's starting to complain that he's hungry."

Laurel didn't budge. In a moderated voice she replied, "Dinner's ready. Jackson and I would love for you and Carl to join us, Donna. There's plenty for everyone."

"Sure smells good," Carl said.

"We wouldn't want to intrude," Donna murmured, still looking at Jackson, unsure and anxious.

Seeming to come to a resolution of some sort, Jackson moved toward her. "Don't be silly, Mom. Laurel and Tyler and I want you to have dinner with us. We'll call it a celebration dinner. After all, he's out of the hospital and our family is all together again."

Donna's eyes flooded, of course, but she managed a smile, probably knowing that neither her son nor her husband would appreciate an emotional scene. "Then we would be delighted to stay."

He leaned over to brush a gentle kiss across her cheek. Laurel knew, as Donna must, that Jackson would need a little more time to come to terms fully with what he had learned, but he was still the same man he had always been. He loved his family, and he would never do anything deliberately to hurt any of them.

No matter how badly he himself had been hurt.

Donna turned to Laurel. "What can I do to help you, dear?"

Normally Laurel would have politely declined any offers of assistance, wanting to prove that she could handle serving dinner on her own. The way she had always done everything else. This time she smiled a bit shyly and replied, "You could help me set the table and put the food out, if you want."

Donna seemed both surprised and pleased that Laurel had actually accepted her help. "Yes," she said. "I'd be happy to do that."

"I'll go get Tyler washed up," Jackson offered, heading for the door.

"I'll help him," Carl said, tagging right behind his son.

"Shirkers," Laurel called after them, making them chuckle in unison as they disappeared.

She didn't usually tease much around her in-laws. With them she was more likely to suppress her natural tendency to be the clown who made people laugh—her way of making them like her. Maybe she'd been secretly afraid that teasing wasn't the way to win her in-laws' affections, and she hadn't known any other way except to be good and quiet and cause them no problems.

Now she believed she had been wrong to hide from them who she really was. There was still a risk that they wouldn't grow to love her, of course, though she and Carl seemed to be off to a good start now. Still she should at least give them a chance to know the real Laurel before they decided how they truly felt about her.

Maybe in being less guarded around her husband and his parents, she could get to know the real Laurel Phillips Reiss a bit better herself.

"It was a nice evening, wasn't it?" Jackson's voice was a low, satisfied rumble in the darkness of their bedroom later that night.

Her cheek on his bare shoulder, Laurel nodded as she remembered the family dinner. Tyler had been the center of everyone's attention, of course, and he'd made the most of it, chattering and performing with uninhibited enthusiasm. His cheeriness had made it easier for the adults to put their issues away and enjoy the meal together.

The usual stilted courtesy between Laurel and her mother-in-law threatened to make an occasional appearance—four years of habit were hard to break, Laurel had discovered—but she had made a determined effort to keep the conversation light and friendly, and Donna had cooperated fully.

The whole evening had been very much what she had always fantasized a family meal should be like during her childhood, when she had spent so many evenings alone eating cereal in front of a television and wondering if her mother would be home before dawn.

Donna had looked much better when she left than when she had arrived, and Carl was grateful enough that he went so far as to kiss Laurel's cheek on his way out. The gesture had been enough to bring an ache to her heart, but it was a pleasant ache.

Jackson and Laurel had spent the rest of the evening playing with Tyler. Together they had tucked him into bed—and then they had retired to their own bed, where they'd made love with the new commitment that made every kiss so much more special.

She was still recovering from the effects of that lovemaking when he cleared his throat and said, "There's something I haven't had a chance to tell you yet today."

Was he going to start talking about Texas again? Because she still hadn't decided if she was ready to leave everything she'd accomplished here—even a budding new relationship with his parents—and move so far away. "What?"

"Someone delivered an envelope to me at the job site today. It was a note from Jack Crosby. I don't know why he chose to approach me that way."

She lifted her head, blinking at him in the shadows, trying to see his expression. "What did it say?"

"Just that he would like to meet me—and you and Tyler, too. He expressed regrets that we haven't met before this, and said he would like the chance to do so now. He said he's glad Tyler's going to be okay, and that he'll make sure his other four kids are warned about the possibility of themselves or their offspring inheriting the condition. And he said there's some more family medical history he could tell me, if I'm interested."

"It sounds very…cordial."

"Exactly. I wouldn't be surprised if he dictated it to a secretary."

"He's a powerful businessman. He's probably accustomed to people doing what he asks."

"He's going to find out I won't be one of the people who jumps at his bidding."

"So you aren't going to meet with him?" she asked, careful to keep any emotion out of her voice.

He hesitated a long while before answering. "I haven't decided yet. I can't say I really want to get mixed up with the Crosbys, but then again, Tyler has the right to know these other relatives. His aunts and uncles and cousins. I don't want to be guilty of the same thing my folks did to me—withholding information that could come back to take him by surprise later."

"How many half siblings do you have?"

"Four, according to the letter, two of each gender. They range in age from six years older than me to four years younger. That's all I know about them."

"You told me once that you always wished you had a brother. Now you have two of them."

"I don't know, Laurel. We're all adults. They grew up together, but I would be a stranger to them. I can't imagine they would welcome me warmly into the fold."

"You never know. They could be delighted to meet their new brother."

"Right. The one who was born somewhere between the four of them, only proving that dear old dad was a philanderer."

"I'm sure they've already dealt with that. Didn't your mother tell you he finally left his wife for another young mistress? I can't imagine they would blame you."

"I keep trying to imagine how I would feel if my dad were the one to show up with an adult son, conceived after he married Mom. I've got to be honest, Laurel, I'm not sure I would throw my arms around the guy."

She couldn't help smiling. "As if that would ever happen. I doubt that Carl has ever even looked at another woman. And I'm not sure you would even *want* any of your brothers to throw their arms around you."

"That might be a little freaky," he admitted with reluctant amusement.

"But aren't you even curious about them?"

"Maybe. A little."

He was, she could tell. But as Carl had said, it was up to Jackson whether he wanted to meet those people who shared his bloodline. She wouldn't push him one way or another.

Snuggling her cheek into his shoulder again, she told herself that it didn't really matter how many other people he brought into their lives. They were truly together now, a team. It was all she had ever really wanted.

Two weeks later Laurel and Jackson met his biological father together. They had left Tyler in the care of Donna and Carl, who were both nervous but resigned about Jackson's decision to meet Jack Crosby.

The meeting took place in Jack's near-palatial home in one of Portland's most exclusive neighborhoods. Laurel tried not to be intimidated when a scarily efficient maid let them in and then escorted them to Jack's private den.

She was struck almost immediately by the physical resemblances between her husband and Jack Crosby. Almost seventy, Jack was still tall and straight. His hair was white, but she would bet it had once been the same dark blond as Jackson's. His eyes were the same bright blue, barely faded by age, and his golfer's tan bespoke a man who enjoyed being outdoors, just as Jackson did.

She wondered if Jackson noticed any of those similarities as he briefly and rather stiffly shook his biological father's extended hand. "Sir."

"Just call me Jack," the older man advised with a little shrug. "There's no need to stand on formalities. And you must be Laurel."

Even at his age, Jack Crosby still had an eye for women, Laurel decided as he gave her a smile and a quick once-over that made her suspect he hadn't missed one detail of her figure. She nodded to confirm her identity.

"Sorry my wife isn't home, but she's out doing the charity-queen thing. Or spending some more of my money. Maybe making a day of it and doing both. Please, make yourselves comfortable." He waved them to a deep leather sofa, taking a leather armchair across from them. "What would you like to drink? Coffee or tea, or something stronger?"

When they both declined Jack steepled his fingers in front of him and took his time studying Jackson's face. "You've a look of your mother about you. She was a beautiful woman."

"She still is."

There was just a hint of warning in Jackson's voice. He made it clear enough that Crosby had better be very careful when he spoke of Donna.

Jack sighed. "I'm not in the habit of apologizing for the things I've done in my life, Jackson. I never pretended to be a saint. But I do have some regrets. Hurting your mother is one of them. She was very special to me, and I treated her very badly. She deserved better."

"Yes, she did," Jackson replied coolly. "And she found it. My dad has been very good to her."

"I met Carl a few times when I was seeing Donna. He's a good man."

"Yes, he is." That edge of warning was back again, Laurel noted.

Jack gave a slight nod to indicate he had received the message that Jackson didn't want to talk about his parents. He reached behind him to a massive desk and picked up a thick manila envelope, which he then handed to Jackson.

"That's the medical history I promised you. I don't think there's anything you have to worry about particularly, now that your boy has been treated, but you'll want to take care of yourself. I've had two heart attacks myself. Too much rich food and cigar smoke, I've been told. Seems like all they let me have these days is lettuce and water."

Both Jackson and Laurel tried to smile at his jest, but Laurel didn't think hers came off any better than her husband's.

Jack's own smile faded quickly. "How is your boy?" he asked after a moment, trying to keep the conversation moving.

This time it was Laurel who answered. "He's doing very well. You would hardly believe that he just had surgery less than a month ago. I, um, brought a picture of him if you would like to see it."

"Yes, I would. Thank you." He studied the recent studio portrait she handed him, his firm mouth tilting into a slight smile again. "Good-looking boy. Looks just like his father."

Laurel glanced at Jackson. "I've always said so."

Jack's expression turned just a bit wistful. "He looks a lot like my oldest boy, Trent, at that age. At least from what I remember."

After handing the photograph back to Laurel, Jack pushed a hand through his hair in a gesture that eerily resembled Jackson's habit.

"That's something else I regret about my life," he confessed. "I never really got to know my kids. Any of them," he added, looking straight at Jackson. "I know I'm a stranger to you, but trust me, your siblings feel much the same way about me. I had another grandson once—Danny's boy. He was kidnapped four years ago when he was just one. They never found him. I'm sorry to say I hardly knew him at all. Danny and his wife never got over the loss. She committed suicide and he's living in Hawaii like a hermit."

Laurel was shocked by that revelation, and she knew Jackson must feel the same way. "I'm so sorry for your son. What a horrible thing to happen to your family."

Jack sighed heavily. "It isn't the first time I've been through a similar experience. Wealthy people have to be extremely careful when it comes to their children, I'm afraid. I told you about Danny's son to warn you to stay on guard with yours from now on, Jackson. Once word gets out that you're my son, and that you've got some money, you'll have to take reasonable precautions."

Jackson frowned. "But I don't have that kind of money. I'm a job foreman for a construction company. I do all right, but it's hardly—"

"As of today, you're a multimillionaire," Jack interrupted. "I've had my attorneys draw up the papers. You're getting the same amount your siblings got when they reached their majority."

Jackson was on his feet now, shaking his head fiercely. "I did not come here for money. I don't even want your money."

Holding up one hand, Jack spoke patiently. "I never said you did. But it's only fair. I'm as much your biological father as I am my other offsprings'. I never did anything else much for them, either, but I made sure they and their kids would be taken care of after I'm gone."

Jackson didn't back down. "Look, I mean it. I don't want it. I wouldn't know what to do with that much money, and I don't deserve anything you've earned. Give it to your other kids, if you want, but I make my own way."

Jack studied him in apparent bemusement while Laurel wondered if she, too, should rise. She was still trying to digest Jack's announcement, still trying to decide how she felt about it. The one thing she knew for certain was that whether Jackson took the money or not, her feelings for her husband would not change.

"You know, you sound just like I remember Carl Reiss," Jack mused. "He raised you to be much like himself, didn't he?"

Jackson answered stiffly. "I'm proud to say that he did."

Jack nodded. "You should be proud. God knows I've done a number on the kids *I* raised. But the deal's already done. The money's already in your name. You can give it away or put it on the ponies or whatever you want, but I'm not taking it back. Your mother told me you've always wanted to start your own construction business. You could do that, have something to pass down to your boy. Or you could come to work for me? No, I didn't think you'd like that idea."

His own construction business. Jackson's dream. For the sake of that dream, Laurel hoped he wouldn't be too hasty about getting rid of this wholly unexpected inheritance.

"Anyway." Jack rose to face his long-lost son. "I've told your siblings about you, and not a one of them expected me to do anything else. Despite the mess Sheila and I made of their home life, they've all turned out okay. They want to meet you—at least Trent and your sisters do. Danny—well, he's not socializing much these days. Trent's taken over the reins of my company and the responsibility of looking out for his younger siblings. He was the first to insist that I make things right for the son I denied for so long."

Jackson was obviously torn by a desire to escape and a reluctant curiosity about his siblings. Laurel suspected he had decided to think about his newfound wealth later, in private.

"You said Danny's a widower," she said to give Jackson time to collect himself. "Are the others married? Do they have children?"

"Trent's divorced. Married himself a manipulative witch just like his mother," Jack added in a mutter of disgust. "He's still smarting over that mistake. Ivy, the youngest, is married to Maxwell von Husden, king of Lantanya. They have an infant son."

"I remember reading about that marriage," Laurel murmured. "It made all the headlines."

Jack nodded, looking almost smug about having royalty in his family. "My other girl's also married and expecting. Katie. The next youngest. She married Peter Logan."

"Leslie Logan's son," Laurel said. She remembered hearing about that union, too. The Crosbys and the Logans had always been fierce business rivals and the gossip columnists had been intrigued by the Romeo-and-Juliet aspect of Katie and Peter's courtship.

"That's who she wanted. Never thought I'd see the day…" He shrugged, then continued. "Anyway, I'd like to give a little reception for you to meet your brothers and sisters, Jackson. Just family. Bring your wife and your boy, and Donna and Carl will be welcome to join us, as well, if they'll come. You can all have a nice time getting to know each other and comparing notes about what a bastard I am."

He sounded almost proud of his reputation, Laurel thought in exasperation. She didn't expect ever to grow as fond of Jackson's biological father as she was of Carl, and she knew Jackson would never have that sort of closeness with Jack Crosby, either. But they were family, and lately she had come to understand just how much that meant.

"I'll think about it," Jackson muttered.

Jack nodded. "You do that. Get back to me soon, though, will you? I'm not getting any younger. I'd like to do something right for my kids before I check out."

A week later Jackson, Laurel and Tyler stood outside the door of Jack Crosby's mansion once again. This time they were there to meet most of the rest of the family, three of his four half-siblings and two spouses Jack had told them about. Donna and Carl had declined the invitation to join them, hardly to Jackson's surprise, but they had encouraged him to go.

"Who knows, Jay," Carl had said, "maybe you'll get to be friends with your brothers, if nothing else. A man can't have too many friends."

Knowing that everyone was waiting inside, and eyeing the extra security guards posted around the property in response to the presence of royalty, Jackson still wasn't sure he wanted to go through with this. What the hell was he supposed to say to a king, even if the guy was his brother-in-law?

He still hadn't sorted out all his feelings about the developments of the past month. Too much had happened at once for him to adjust to the changes easily.

He was slowly coming around to the idea of owning his own business. Jack had hit an emotional bull's-eye when he had mentioned that Jackson could leave the company to his son someday, something he'd always hoped to be able to do. He could do a few other things with the money, too, like helping Beverly go to nursing school, as a way of thanking her for practically saving his son's life. But he still didn't think of himself as a multimillionaire. That was going to take a little more time.

"Are you okay?" Laurel asked, giving his arm a slight squeeze.

He turned to face her. She was so beautiful tonight, her dark-blond hair swept into a sophisticated twist, her slender body showcased to perfection in a little black dress that she'd obsessed over before finally deciding it would do. She'd bought it on sale—a habit she wouldn't break any time soon. She hadn't gotten used to the idea of wealth, either.

It pleased him to know that she would still be by his side regardless of whether he had accepted the money or given it to the first charity that had popped into his mind. As she had pointed out when they'd discussed it, he hadn't had any money when she'd married him. He hadn't had much more when they had renewed their confessions of love only a few weeks ago. Now that he did have money, nothing had changed between them.

They had come a long way in a very short time, he was pleased to note. The love had been there all along. It had just taken a couple of crises to make them see how foolish they had both been to risk letting it slip away from them.

"I'm fine," he said. "I love you, Laurel Reiss."

She smiled in surprise and pleasure. "I love you, too, Jackson Reiss."

He leaned down to brush his lips across hers, taking care not to smudge the lipstick she had applied so painstakingly.

"Daddy?" Tyler tugged at his coat. "Are we going in to meet the new people?"

Giving Laurel one last, quick peck, Jackson leaned down to scoop his son into his arms. "Yeah, sport. We're going in. As a team," he added for Laurel's benefit.

And then he reached out to press the doorbell.

Epilogue

Everett Baker crumpled the newspaper he'd been reading between his hands, which shook with emotions he couldn't have described had he tried. The society section today had been filled with news of Jack Crosby's acknowledgment of his long-lost son.

Apparently, Jackson Reiss had been welcomed into the Crosby family with open arms—and a substantial monetary endowment. Even one of the Logans had been in attendance at the reception in Jackson's honor—Peter. The one who had been adopted after Terrence and Leslie Logan's son was kidnapped and who was now married to Katie Crosby.

Everett wondered how everyone would react if they were to discover that the Crosbys weren't the only ones with a long-lost son in their midst. Would *he* be welcomed so warmly? He was hardly the fine, upstanding citizen Jackson Reiss was reported to be, but, then, he hadn't had the advantage of being raised by loving, supportive parents, had he?

He wondered if anyone would understand what the kind of upbringing he'd suffered could do to a boy who had been wrenched from his adoring parents. If they could accept him for what he had become…

He spent a few minutes fantasizing about a reception in his honor given by the Logan family. And then he shook his head in impatience at his foolish and highly unlikely daydreaming. Not every man was as lucky as Jackson Reiss, he reminded himself. Not everyone had every wrong made right with a nice dinner and a hefty check.

Some people had to find their own way in the world. And Everett Baker—born Robbie Logan—was one of those determined souls.

*Turn the page for a sneak preview
of the next emotional* LOGAN'S LEGACY *title,*
THE NEWLYWEDS

by USA TODAY *bestselling author Elizabeth Bevarly
On sale in March 2005...*

Sam glanced around at his surroundings again, his gaze halting when it fell on Bridget Logan. Too much beauty, he thought again. He would have thought such a thing wasn't possible. But with that thick mane of dark-red hair that even her braid couldn't contain, and with those huge green eyes, and that lush mouth and a body so full of curves only the most expert driver could handle it—then again, Sam had always been an *excellent* driver.... Well. Suffice it to say she was just so damned dazzling, it almost hurt to look at her. Looking at her made him remember all the dreams and hopes and desires he'd embraced as a younger man, things he knew now that he'd never have.

And the hell of it was, she wasn't even at her best. Even travel-rumpled and exhausted, she'd managed to take his breath away when she'd walked up to him in the airport. So much so, that he'd forgotten himself for a moment, had introduced himself simply as Sam Jones, instead of Special Agent Samuel Jones.

And there was a big difference between the two men. Sam Jones was the guy who spent his weekends in blue jeans and sweatshirts, hiking in the Cascades and kayaking on the Willamette, and coaching Little League for the Boys and Girls Club downtown. Sam Jones liked reading Raymond Chandler and watching college basketball and tipping a few with his friends at Foley's Bar and Grill in the blue-collar neighborhood where he'd grown up and still lived.

Special Agent Samuel Jones, on the other hand, was the man who put on nondescript suits Monday through Friday and investigated interstate crimes and helped put scumbags in cages, where they belonged. Agent Jones was focused, driven, no-nonsense and effective. He always concentrated on the job, and he got the job done right.

It was important that he keep Sam Jones and Special Agent Samuel Jones separate. And it was essential that he be the former when he was relaxing and the latter when he was working. That was the only way he could keep himself sane in the face of the viciousness and violence of some of the crimes he investigated.

And even if this case wasn't especially violent, he still had to keep those two men separate. Because Special Agent Samuel Jones was suddenly feeling a lot like Sam Jones, looking at the woman with him not as Special Agent Bridget Logan, who also had a job to do, but as a beautiful, desirable woman he might want to get to know better. And he couldn't allow himself to think about Agent Logan in any terms other than the professional. Not just because he didn't care for her personally—and he was having a hell of a problem warming up to her professionally, too, truth be told—but because that just wasn't the way he operated. Not as an agent. And not as a man. He and Logan had a job to do. Period. And they would do it. Period. And then they'd go their separate ways and never see each other again.

Period.

"Wow, this place is unbelievable," she said now as she turned to look at him, surprising him both because she'd just echoed his own initial thoughts about the place—well, pretty much—and because she could be so impressed by what he would have thought was an unremarkable environment to her.

She stood in the middle of the big living room, bathed in the warm golden glow of a lamp that had already been on when they entered. Pennington had told them that someone from the Bureau had been in earlier to prepare the house for their residence, supplying some basic groceries and turning on the house's heat and such. They'd obviously remembered lights, too, knowing it would be dark—or nearly so—by the time they arrived. The soft light brought out flecks of amber amid the red in Logan's hair, and made her complexion seem almost radiant. He wondered if her eyes would be as luminous and was tempted to draw closer to her to find out.

And just what the hell was he doing, thinking words like *warm* and *amber* and *radiant* and *luminous* in relation to her? He berated himself. He and Logan were *working,* for God's sake. That was the only word he need to be thinking about right now.

"You think so?" he asked, feigning blandness. But he did allow himself to stride farther into the room, halting when only a couple of feet of space lay between them. Wow. In this light, her eyes really were kind of lumi— "I would have thought it was a lot like the place where you grew up," he hurried to add. "I mean, the house you showed me as being your parents' looked even bigger than this one."

She seemed to give his comment some thought before replying, but then she nodded. "Yeah, our house was a little bigger, maybe, but my parents were more minimalist when it came to furnishings. I mean, our house didn't have nearly this much color or this much…" She threw her arms open wide, and he tried not to notice how the gesture caused her breasts to strain against her white shirt enough that he could see the outline of her bra beneath, and how it looked sort of pink and lacy. "…stuff," she concluded. "Everything in this house is just so…so extravagant. Where did the Bureau find this place, anyway?"

Sam had wondered that himself when he'd first looked at the house yesterday, but, like a good agent, he didn't question authority. "I don't know," he said honestly. "It may be a house the federal government owns that they keep for visiting dignitaries. Or they may have made arrangements with a homeowner who isn't using it right now because they're working overseas or taking an extended vacation. It might have even been confiscated for tax evasion. Ours is not to question why," he told her.

"Yeah, and we never do, do we?" she asked.

And Sam wasn't sure, but he thought he detected just a hint of sarcasm in the question. Well, my, my, my. Maybe Golden Girl Logan wasn't such a perfect little agent, after all.

"Can we go over this thing one more time?" she asked. "I'm sorry—usually once is enough for me, but I haven't slept in over twenty-four hours, and my brain is just having some trouble processing everything Pennington told me. We're a just-married couple, right?" she began without even waiting for his okay.

"Right," Sam told her. "We're the newlyweds. We met in the fall, then eloped a month ago because we were so wildly in love. We just recently surprised your family with the news, and that's why there was no talk of our marriage around town before now. At the time we married, we were living in the Washington, D.C., area, but I put my house up for sale and you listed your condo right after the wedding, because we knew we'd be moving to Portland after we married. I'm bringing my business headquarters out here so we can be closer to your family—that's my wedding present to you."

"Well, aren't you the generous spouse, relocating your entire business on your trophy wife's behalf?" Logan asked with a smile. And strangely, she seemed to be teasing him when she did. Sam told himself he was just imagining it. It was *not* wishful thinking.

"Well, I am a wealthy steel baron, after all," he told her. "I can afford to be generous. Besides, from what I hear, I just dote on my trophy wife and would do anything to indulge her." And where the prospect of playing that role had made him feel like a complete sucker a few days ago, suddenly, for some reason, it didn't seem nearly as distasteful now.

"So that's how you made your reeking piles of filthy lucre," she said. Still smiling. Still seeming to be teasing him. And Sam still told himself he was only imagining it and not thinking wishfully. "You're a steel baron." She tilted her head to the side and studied him. "Which is going to make this role even more interesting to play—not to mention more challenging—since I've never really been a woman who went for the big-business-mogul type."

No, what was interesting—never mind challenging—Sam thought, was how badly he wanted to ask her just what type she *did* really go for. Especially since she came from a family full of big-business-mogul types, and seemed to be the kind of woman who had been groomed to marry just such a man. Then again, maybe that was precisely why she didn't go for them. Tamping down his curiosity, he kept his question to himself. That was none of his business. And it wouldn't be in any way helpful for working the case.

In spite of his self-admonition, however—and much to his own horror—he heard himself ask her, "Are you saying you didn't think anyone will buy the idea of your being attracted to me, Logan?"

Her eyes widened at that, and her smile fell. And she didn't seem to be teasing at all now, when she said, "Of course not. My God, any woman would be—" But she cut herself off before finishing whatever she had intended to say, her cheeks burning bright pink at whatever had inspired her to say it.

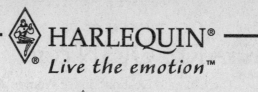

Harlequin Historicals®
Historical Romantic Adventure!

From rugged lawmen and valiant knights to defiant heiresses and spirited frontierswomen, Harlequin Historicals will capture your imagination with their dramatic scope, passion and adventure.

*Harlequin Historicals...
they're too good to miss!*

HARLEQUIN®
INTRIGUE®

WE'LL LEAVE YOU BREATHLESS!

If you've been looking for thrilling tales of
contemporary passion and sensuous love stories
with taut, edge-of-the-seat suspense—then
you'll love Harlequin Intrigue!

Every month, you'll meet six new heroes
who are guaranteed to make your spine tingle
and your pulse pound. With them you'll enter
into the exciting world of Harlequin Intrigue—
where your life is on the line
and so is your heart!

THAT'S INTRIGUE—
ROMANTIC SUSPENSE
AT ITS BEST!

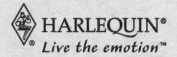

HARLEQUIN®
Live the emotion™